ANIMAL ALERT
CRASH

Animal Alert series

1 Intensive Care
2 Abandoned
3 Killer on the Loose
4 Quarantine
5 Skin and Bone
6 Crash
7 Blind Alley

ANIMAL
ALERT

CRASH

Jenny Oldfield

*Hodder
Children's
Books*

a division of Hodder Headline plc

**Special thanks to David Brown and Margaret Marks of Leeds
RSPCA Animal Home and Clinic, and to Raj Duggal M.V.Sc.,
M.R.C.V.S. and Louise Kinvig B.V.M.S., M.R.C.V.S.**

First published in Great Britain in 1998
by Hodder Children's Books

British Library Cataloguing in Publication Data
A record for this book is available from the British Library

ISBN 0 340 70869 7

Typeset by Avon Dataset Ltd, Bidford-on-Avon, Warks

Printed and bound in Great Britain by
Mackays of Chatham plc, Chatham, Kent

Hodder Children's Books
A division of Hodder Headline plc
338 Euston Road
London NW1 3BH

1

'Tell me exactly how to find you!' Carly Grey took the emergency phone call before evening surgery. She scribbled down the address. '14 Church Street. That's off City Road, isn't it?'

Steve Winter, the Beech Hill inspector, leaned on the reception desk and listened in. He picked up the tension in her voice.

'By St Martin's Church? OK, I've got that. We'll be there as soon as we can.' Carly tried to keep things calm, though the boy's voice on the other end of the phone was obviously upset.

1

'Hurry! She's bleeding and she can't stand up!'

'Don't try to move her. Wait for us.'

'She's still lying in the road. There's a big traffic jam.'

'Never mind. Don't touch her. Just put something over her to keep her warm.' Carly looked up at Steve, who was reaching for his jacket. She gave first aid advice as quickly as she could. 'You can stop the bleeding with a wad of cloth. Press hard.'

'I'll try.' The young voice wavered.

'Have you got someone with you?'

'My mum sent me to phone you. She's still with Bubble.'

'OK, go and tell her we're on our way!' Carly put down the phone and ran to join Steve at the door. 'Road traffic accident. The casualty is a long-haired grey cat.'

'Not *another* RTA!' He ran ahead, across the carpark, with Carly following. 'On Church Street? That's the third cat we've dealt with this month.'

'Aren't we going in the van?' She watched him open the back doors and reach for his bag.

2

'At this time of day it'll probably be quicker by foot,' he decided. 'Rush hour. Everybody coming home from work.'

St Martin's Church was a kilometre up the main road away from the city centre. Cars would be queuing nose to tail. So they ran up Beech Hill, dodging pedestrians and using the crossings to beat the jam. The minutes ticked by as they passed the supermarket, then the pine furniture shop, the hairdresser's and the off-licence.

'Hey, don't shove!' a woman cried, as Carly tried to nip through a gap on the crowded pavement.

'Sorry!' She was out of breath, ahead of Steve, who had to carry his heavy bag. A hundred metres down the road she could see a turnoff by the church, and a small knot of people gathered by the kerb. 'There!' She glanced over her shoulder and waited for Steve to catch up. Then she drew a deep breath and ploughed on through the crowd.

'Watch it!' another voice complained.

'. . . No need to push!'

'. . . What's going on?'

Steve and Carly ignored the protests. They must get to the scene of the accident before it was too late.

'Excuse me, could you please move to one side!' Steve spoke up as they elbowed through the onlookers. The crowd gave way reluctantly to his official uniform. 'Come on, Carly, through here!' It was his turn to wait as she squeezed between two parked cars. 'That's right, stand well back. Give us room to see what we're doing.'

Carly ducked and dodged bulky shopping bags and briefcases. She was small and slight enough to get through after Steve. In the space in the centre of the crowd, she saw a young woman with beaded hair and a boy of about eight huddled over a cat in the gutter. The woman held a bloodstained handkerchief in one hand. Glancing at her watch, Carly saw that it had taken her and Steve ten minutes to reach the scene.

'You're too late,' the woman whispered as they arrived. She slumped forward and sighed. 'I think she's dead.'

The book shook his head. 'No, Mum, she can't be!'

'Let's see, shall we!' Gently, Steve parted them and knelt beside the victim. It was a long-haired, dark-grey cat lying in a pool of blood.

Carly crouched and waited as Steve felt for a pulse on the inside of the cat's thigh. 'Still alive,' he told them. Her eyes were closed and she hardly seemed to be breathing. 'Carly, give me a pad of cotton wool from the bag, and try to find a sheet in the bottom section. That's right, as quick as you can.'

'See, she's not dead!' the boy whispered. 'They're going to save her life!' He was sobbing with relief as his mother drew him away.

Carly passed Steve the cotton wool. 'Shall I loosen her collar?'

He nodded. 'Her breathing's pretty irregular. When you've done that, I want you to hold this pad against her ribs while I open her mouth and take a look inside.' He leaned forward and eased open the cat's jaws.

Suddenly she jerked and struggled.

'Sorry, I didn't mean to hurt you.' Steve waited for the cat to calm down. He told Carly to keep the pad of cotton wool in place. 'She's weak from loss of blood, and I think the jaw may be broken. What hit her?' he asked the woman.

'A motor-bike. It drove right over her and didn't even stop. It went up over the pavement and almost crashed into the churchyard wall. Then it just drove on. We live in the flat above the betting shop opposite. Jordan saw it all.' She held her son's hand and watched anxiously.

'I'm going to try again,' Steve warned Carly. 'We need to see what's stopping her breathing.'

Carly nodded. She held her own breath as she kept the pad pressed against the bleeding wound and Steve eased the cat's mouth open again. This time, there was no struggle.

'As far as I can tell, there's no foreign body in there blocking the air passage.' He felt gently with his finger, hooking it inside the mouth and flattening the cat's tongue. 'This should do the trick.'

Carly shuddered as blood and saliva trickled to the ground.

'Poor thing!' someone in the crowd groaned.

The little boy cried out loud. 'Don't let her die!'

Steve twisted the cat's head so that her mouth

emptied and she drew a shuddering breath. 'We need to get her back to Beech Hill!' he told Carly. 'Come what may!'

'Are you sure you should move her? What if she's got broken bones!' The motor-bike had obviously been going fast. The cat was badly injured.

'We'll have to risk it. If we don't get her into the surgery to resuscitate her, she won't stand a chance.' He took the sheet and spread it on the ground.

Carly understood that it was a life-or-death situation. She waited for Steve's next instruction.

'OK, you slip the sheet under her as I lift her up a bit. Ready? Go!'

She slid it into place, seeing a red stain appear on the clean green sheet as it soaked up blood from the ground. The cat wasn't moving, but lay limp in Steve's hands. Gently he eased her down on to the sheet. 'Good. Now, I'm going to hold this end, and you hold the other, so we've got her in a kind of hammock. Ready to lift?'

They stood up smoothly, with the patient hidden inside the makeshift sling. Steve nodded and swiftly told Jordan and his mother to come with them to Beech Hill. 'Can you help your mum to carry my bag?' he asked the boy.

Bravely holding back his tears, the boy nodded.

'Let's go!' Steve led the way, and this time the crowd parted smoothly to let them through, sensing the urgency.

'Good luck,' someone said, going on ahead to press the button at a nearby pedestrian crossing. 'I hope she makes it!'

Carly nodded. 'So do I!'

She kept a firm hold of her end of the sheet as they hurried back the way they had come. This was a bad accident and they were going to need more than luck to pull the cat through, she knew.

'Skeletal and soft tissue damage,' Steve reported to Paul Grey as they reached the Rescue Centre and took the cat inside. 'Her breathing is erratic, but her ribs are injured, so I haven't been able to give artificial respiration.'

Carly's dad took in the situation at a glance. 'Take her through to theatre,' he told them. 'We'll get her on a respirator straight away.'

All heads in the waiting room were turned their way as Carly and Steve rushed across reception. Jordan and his mother followed close after, but Bupinda stepped out from behind the desk as the doors into the operating theatre swung open. 'It's best if you wait here,' she told them quietly. 'She's in good hands.'

Carly felt the door close behind her. Ahead lay the prep room where the vets assessed patients for surgery. Steel instruments and rubber oxygen masks hung in racks and the examination table was scrubbed spotless. Tiled white walls gleamed under the glare of spotlights.

As they lay the patient on the table and took away the soiled sheet, Paul Grey took a mask from its hook and placed it gently over the cat's face. Then he turned on the oxygen supply. 'What happened?'

'She was run over by a motor-bike on Church Street.' Carly watched anxiously for signs of life.

Her dad tutted. 'It's a real black spot. How many RTAs have we had from that junction with City Road?'

'This is the third.' *Don't remind me*, she thought. The two other cats had died. 'Her name's Bubble. What kind of cat is she?'

'She looks like pure Norwegian Forest to me.' Paul cast an expert eye over the long, thick coat and bushy tail. 'Don't worry, they may look cuddly, but they're a tough breed.'

But Carly did still worry. 'Is she breathing any better?'

Gently Paul took the cat's pulse. 'Her heartbeat's stronger. That's a good sign. And she seems to be coming round; look!'

Behind the oxygen mask, Bubble stirred. Her head twitched and her amber eyes flickered open. She looked up at the glaring lights and staring faces.

'We need to keep her still.' Carly's dad took away the mask and moved quickly to give the cat a pain-killing injection. 'You see the torn nails on the front feet?'

She nodded.

'That's usually evidence that a cat has been in a traffic accident. And this injury to the left side looks bad to me. What's probably happened is that at least one of the ribs is broken.' He glanced round the room. 'Fetch Melanie, would you?'

Carly ran to find the nurse, who brought admission forms from the office. Jordan and his mother had already given her more information; Bubble was three years old, a pedigree as Paul had thought. 'The little boy's very upset,' she told them. 'His mum is trying to prepare him for the worst, but he seems to think we can perform miracles.'

'Sound medical practice, yes,' Paul said quietly. He was preparing a drip containing fluid to counteract shock. 'Miracles; they're much harder to do!'

'Try telling that to a scared eight-year-old.' Melanie went ahead with her part of the job. She shaved a small patch on the cat's front leg with an electric razor and rubbed the skin clean ready for the needle attached to a narrow tube. Soon they had the patient hooked up to the drip. A shot of antibiotics was next on the list.

Carly stood back out of the way. She and Steve had done everything they could. Now it was up to her dad and Mel. The idea calmed her, and she breathed more easily, knowing that he was one of the best vets around. She watched the nurse take a pair of tweezers and begin to pick dirt out of the wound, holding Bubble's paws out of the way as she worked. Then her dad took his stethoscope and listened.

'It's what I was afraid of,' he confirmed, frowning as he concentrated. 'A rib has punctured the lung. We need to put a needle in through the chest wall to syringe out the air that's got trapped in the tissue surrounding the lung.'

Once more Carly shuddered. Perhaps they shouldn't have brought Bubble from the scene of the accident after all? Moving her could have made the damage much worse. The poor cat lay gazing up at the lights, dazed and too weak to move.

'What a pity. She's a beautiful creature.' Mel went back to picking out dirt. There was a deep frown on her usually cheerful face. 'It makes me mad!'

'What does?' Steve stood at the door of the prep room, suddenly alert.

'Tell you later.' The nurse was too busy to

12

explain. She finished cleaning the wound, then carefully covered the patient with a soft, clean towel.

'That's right, keep her warm,' Paul agreed. 'She may need surgery later, but I think we've done all we can for now.' He stood back and began to peel off his surgical gloves.

'What about X-rays?' Carly didn't want them to stop. If Bubble had broken ribs and possibly a broken jaw, shouldn't they operate straight away?

'Tomorrow, when she recovers from the trauma of the accident,' her father told her firmly. He unhooked his green surgical apron and ditched it in the waste-bin.

'*If!*' Mel was keen to warn Carly not to expect too much. 'If she recovers from the shock.'

'She will.' Carly tried to ignore the warning. 'Dad says this is a tough breed.'

'Tough or not, she's in a critical condition,' Mel insisted.

For a moment the nurse's outspoken comment stopped everyone in their tracks.

Steve hesitated, one hand on the door, ready to

go and talk to Bubble's owners in reception. Paul looked up from jotting down notes on the admission card.

Carly gazed down at the patient hooked up to a drip, lying motionless under the warm cover. Bubble's face peeped out from the towel, the third eyelids masking her brilliant almond-shaped eyes, her smoky fur matted with blood. She heard Melanie press the point home.

'If this cat makes it through the night, we'll definitely be talking miracles!' she said.

2

'Bubble *is* going to get better, isn't she?' Jordan Smith sat in Steve Winter's chair in the Beech Hill office. Bupinda had given the cat's owners a quiet, private room to listen to Paul Grey's verdict.

'We're not sure.' Carly's dad spoke carefully, sitting on the edge of the desk beside Jordan. 'We're looking after her in a special place called an intensive care unit. That means she can stay connected to tubes and wires that will help her stay alive.'

The boy stared up at the vet with wide, dark eyes. His round, brown face was streaked with tears. 'What sort of wires?'

'Wires that are taped to her skin to help us see that her heart is beating properly. The heartbeat shows up on a screen as a kind of wavy line. As long as the wiggly line in the monitor is nice and even, it means that Bubble is doing OK. Would you like to come and see?'

'No!' Quickly he shook his head and hid his face behind his hands. Beneath the sporty red T-shirt and black jogging trousers, Jordan was a very scared little boy.

'Maybe tomorrow.' His mother, Tina, moved in and put her arm around his shoulder. 'It's wonderful what they can do,' she promised. 'You wait and see!'

'I hear you were the one who telephoned for help?' Paul changed the subject.

Jordan sniffed and managed to look up. 'How do you know that?'

'Carly told me. She said you explained what had happened really clearly. That was great.'

Carly smiled and nodded. 'It was. Without

you, Bubble wouldn't have got the help she needed.'

'You hear that?' The purple and white beads in Tina Smith's long hair clicked as she bent to give her son a hug. 'Wait till I tell your dad what a star you were!'

The boy sniffed again. A proud smile crept across his face, but the praise didn't quite wipe away the picture of his beloved cat being carried away in a blood-soaked sling. 'She's really sick, isn't she, Mum?'

'But look how well she's being cared for. It's gonna be OK, Jordan, you wait!' Mrs Smith stood him up, ready to leave. 'When we come and see her tomorrow, she'll be much better.'

Carly glanced at her dad, wondering what he would say. Mel's warning words still echoed in her head.

'You can ring us whenever you like to check on how Bubble is doing.' Paul showed them out of the office to the main door. He had a waiting room full of patients, but he hadn't rushed the Smiths away until they were ready. 'Even if you ring out of surgery hours, the call will be put through to Carly and me in the flat upstairs.'

Tina took Jordan by the hand and nodded. 'Thanks for everything.' She smiled over Paul's shoulder at Carly and Steve.

'Don't thank us yet,' Paul said quietly. He took Bubble's admission card out of his pocket and checked the details. 'We've got your telephone number. We'll give you a ring if there's any news.'

As Tina walked her little boy across the car-park and Bupinda called the first patient into a treatment room, Carly saw a familiar figure come through the gates. Or two familiar figures, if she counted Vinny. Vinny was a bow-legged, barrel-chested, black, brown and white mongrel that belonged to her friend, Hoody. Hoody loped along. He was as tall and skinny as Vinny was broad and squat. With his spiky haircut and narrowed brown eyes, he liked people to think he was hard. It was a good act; until Carly had got to know him, she would have run a mile rather than talk to him.

'Hi, Hoody!' she called now. 'Have you come to ask about our maths homework?'

It was mid-October; the end of half term, but still the whole weekend ahead.

'You what?' He stopped dead, while Vinny trotted on to greet Carly.

'Joke,' she said. Hoody never got his homework in on time. 'You know, ha-ha!'

'Yeah, very funny.' He frowned.

She bent to stroke the dog. 'So?'

'So, what?' The frown deepened.

'If it's not homework, why are you here?'

'Has there got to be a reason?' He shrugged.

'Do you always answer a question with a question?' Carly grinned.

'Yeah. Why?'

'See!' She enjoyed teasing him. 'Seriously, though, I'm busy. It's evening surgery.'

'I know. I came to take a dog for a walk.' Hoody pushed through the door, heading towards the kennels at the back of the surgery, where they housed the strays and cruelty cases that Steve brought in. 'Which one shall I take?'

'The Old English sheepdog in number six.' Carly followed him down the corridor. She knew that the big dog needed plenty of exercise. 'His name's Bob. Watch out for him; he can pull your arm out of its socket.'

'Why's he here?' Hoody knew his way around. He went straight to the right kennel and unlocked the door. A giant grey and white ball of fur flew out in a flurry of barks and bounds. 'Whoa! Watch it!'

Carly laughed as the dog swamped Hoody. 'His owner couldn't handle him. Said he wrecked the garden, then started on the furniture in the house. Gave her a nervous breakdown, so she sent him to us to find him a new home. Personally, I think it was the woman who gave Bob a breakdown.'

At last Hoody managed to get the dog on the lead. Vinny sat by the door, head to one side, with what looked like a smile on his blunt face. 'What's this I heard about a cat being run over?' Hoody asked.

'News travels fast round here.' She led the way back into reception.

'Yeah, well, it only caused a traffic jam a kilo-metre long down the main road, didn't it?' Hanging round on street corners and cruising through the housing estates with Vinny in tow meant Hoody was usually the first to pick up what was going on. Now he hung on to the sheepdog, determined to pick up more news. 'I heard it was pretty bad. Did it die?'

'No!' She folded her arms and leaned back against the desk.

'Not yet,' Mel muttered. She'd overheard while she was looking through a drawer of file cards in the office. Now she stuck her head out to join in. 'But it does make me mad, like I said!'

'What does? The motor-bike driving off without even stopping?' Hoody had heard this much already.

'Well, that gets me, of course.' Mel was ready for a quick gossip. She came out, swinging her curly red ponytail behind her shoulder, stabbing a Biro into the air to make her point. But no, what I really meant was, this is the third time this has happened in as many weeks.'

'So? It's a busy road.' Hoody didn't see the point. He struggled to hold an impatient Bob back from his walk.

'No busier than it was six months ago, or even

three months, and we didn't get all these accidents then, did we?'

Carly stopped to think. 'No. That's a point.'

'Exactly. I live down there, so I should know.' Mel paused to check that she wasn't needed in the treatment rooms. When she came back, she spelled it out for them. 'What I'm saying is, suddenly we get all these accidents with cats being run over. Last time, the car involved drove into a tree outside the church and crashed.'

'I remember that. It was in the paper. One cat shot over the churchyard wall, chased by another one. It ran under the car wheels and got killed straight off.' Hoody's memory was sharp.

'So?' It was Carly's turn to ask.

'So, how come so many cats are being lured into the churchyard all of a sudden?' Mel opened her eyes wide.

'What do you mean, "lured"?' Hoody grappled with Bob to make him sit.

'Enticed. Tempted across the busy road in the middle of rush hour. It never used to happen!'

'You mean, there's some strange new attraction?' Carly was puzzled.

'Well, there must be, mustn't there?' To Mel it was obvious. 'And what could it be, to make all these cats risk life and limb by crossing the road? It's only an old churchyard over that wall, and an empty church.'

'Mice?' Hoody suggested. 'Since they boarded that place up, I bet it's full of them.'

Carly knew that St Martin's Church had closed twelve months earlier. It was a huge place with a tall steeple, blackened by over a century of grime and fumes. The churchyard was full of broken gravestones and overgrown mounds, and the whole place had a sad, spooky air. 'Could be,' she said thoughtfully. A disused church could be a real draw for cats on the prowl.

'But why so many?' Mel wasn't satisfied. 'There's dozens of these cats heading across the road.'

'Dozens?' Carly frowned.

'Yes. You see them dodging the traffic all day long. They bob up on to the wall and disappear into the long grass in the graveyard. I've seen owners trying to get them back before they vanish, but the cats are too busy tracking down these mice or whatever to take any notice.'

'We don't know that it's mice.' Carly didn't go for Hoody's theory.

'Have you got a better idea?' A determined look had come over him; he bunched up his mouth and crossed his forehead into a frown.

Carly admitted that she hadn't. She heard Liz Hutchins, the assistant vet at Beech Hill, call her from treatment room two. 'But it would be good if we found out for sure.' She dropped a hint before hurrying off, not knowing if Hoody would take her up on it.

He shrugged. Then, holding on to the giant dog, he loped off with Vinny.

Inside the treatment room, Carly found a strange sight that took her mind off the Church Street cat problem. Liz was scratching her head over what looked like a large steel drum with tubes and wires hanging out of it. It was part of a machine, but what it was doing sitting on the treatment table Carly couldn't imagine.

'Don't even ask!' Liz raised her eyebrows. A worried, bald-headed man in overalls stood nearby. 'It's the innards of a washing machine.'

'What's it doing here?' Carly did ask. She moved closer to peer inside the drum.

'Mr Bateman had better tell you himself.' The young vet shook her head and stood with hands on hips.

'Georgina's in there,' the man explained. 'At least, we think she is.'

'Who's Georgina?' Carly could see nothing except shiny metal and holes where the water drained out of the drum.

'My granddaughter Millie's pet gerbil.'

Carly gasped. 'Her gerbil's got into your washing-machine?'

'According to my wife. We're looking after Georgina while Millie's on holiday with her mum and dad.' The old man paused and sighed. 'It was a couple of days ago. My wife had decided to give the cage a good clean. Georgina was happily nibbling raisins on the kitchen worktop. Joan just turned her back for a few seconds, and she was gone!'

'But what makes you think she's in here!' Carly couldn't believe that he'd taken the washing-machine to bits to bring part of it into the surgery.

25

'We looked everywhere else. We were just about to give up and nip to the pet shop to buy a new one before Millie came home, hoping she wouldn't notice the difference, when we heard this tiny scrabbling noise inside the machine.'

'Lucky you hadn't done any washing!' Liz was still stuck over what to do.

Carly gave a small grin, then coughed to make herself be serious. 'Are you *sure* she's stuck in there?'

'Afraid so.' The old man sighed. 'As a matter of fact, I don't hold out much hope for the poor little thing. She was making plenty of noise until I started working on the machine to try and get her out. But she's gone quiet these last couple of hours.'

'Hmm.' Liz didn't like the sound of this. 'When a gerbil goes quiet it could mean she's having a seizure – a sort of epileptic fit. It's quite common.'

'And serious?' Carly had her head almost inside the drum. She listened hard.

'Quite often fatal. It happens especially when they're scared.'

'Can you see anything in there?' Mr Bateman craned anxiously over the table.

'No – wait; yes! I think I can see her!' Carly had spotted something brown inside one of the drainage holes. 'The problem is, these holes are too small to get my fingers down.' She poked gently and felt a patch of soft fur. 'She's definitely in here!'

'Can you take the back off this drum?' Liz asked.

The old man nodded and took some tools out of his overalls pocket. He worked quickly to remove a metal plate.

'Now, can you reach inside from the back?' Liz asked Carly.

'Gently does it!' Mr Bateman urged.

Carly stretched her slim hand inside two layers of metal until she could feel the gerbil's soft shape. 'She's not moving!' she whispered. 'But she's still warm at least.'

'Pull her out,' Liz decided, standing by with a soft paper towel.

So Carly hooked her fingers around the trapped animal and pulled gently. Slowly she eased Georgina out of the machine until the gerbil came into view.

'Well done!' Mr Bateman sighed.

The tiny, golden animal crouched in Carly's palm. Her big eyes stared and her ears and whiskers twitched.

'Good, she's not had a seizure.' Liz took her and wrapped her in the towel. 'In fact, she looks in pretty good shape, considering.'

Carly breathed out. 'She was fooling us!' Georgina looked perky enough after her ordeal. Her sharp little black claws pawed free of the towel as she scrabbled to get out.

'Let's put her down and see.' Liz placed her on the table and surrounded her with a pile of paper tissues. Soon Georgina was burrowing happily into the pile. 'She's fine!'

'Hungry, I expect.' Carly realised that the gerbil couldn't have eaten for two days.

Mr Bateman promised to get her straight back home. 'We'll soon have her tucking into a dish of porridge. That's her favourite.' He looked pleased to have rescued the precious family pet as he took instructions from Liz about how to look after her on the journey home.

But for Carly there was no time to enjoy their success.

'Carly, could you go to room one?' Bupinda called over the intercom.

Her dad needed her next door. They treated a black-and-white rabbit for ear mange. 'And while we're at it, we'll give his claws a trim,' Paul decided.

Then there were the dogs in the kennels to feed. Hoody brought Bob back from his walk as Carly set down the metal dishes for each dog. The big sheepdog almost pulled him over as it rushed for its supper.

But soon all the dogs were busily feeding, nosing their dishes across the concrete floor, snuffling for bits they might have missed.

'Time to check on Bubble.' Carly was out in the corridor when she remembered the puzzle about the cats on Church Street. 'Did you go and find out?'

'Where? I'm not a mind-reader, you know.'

'Sorry. Church Street. *Is* it mice?'

Hoody shrugged. 'How could I? I was taking

Bob for a walk, wasn't I?' He chewed his lip. 'Tomorrow's Saturday. We could both go.'

Carly stared at him. 'You want me to come?' Usually Hoody went off and did things alone. He never invited her along.

'I just asked you, didn't I?'

She went on staring. What had got into him?

'Nine o'clock. I'll see you there.' He whistled Vinny and set off past her, without waiting for an answer.

'Right.' It came out too quietly for him to have heard.

But, as she got over the surprise, she knew she would definitely be there in the morning. *Why?* She asked herself the question as she went upstairs to intensive care.

The answer came with a second jolt of surprise – partly because she wanted to solve the mystery of the reckless cats. And partly because Hoody had actually lowered his guard and asked her for help.

3

Bubble had been on her drip and hooked up to a monitor for over two hours when Carly dropped in to check how she was. She found her dad there, taking readings from the screen and looking closely into the plastic cage at the injured cat.

'How is she?'

'Just about hanging on. Her blood pressure's pretty low, though.'

Bubble lay on her side, legs outstretched. Her thick grey coat was still matted with dry blood, and the needles and tubes strapped to her small body made Carly glad that Jordan had chosen not to come up to see her before he left.

'Shall I try to clean her up?' Carly herself could hardly bear to look at the sorry state she was in.

'No. Best not to handle her for the time being.' Paul sounded weary after a busy surgery. 'What she needs now is peace and quiet.'

On the wall behind them, a clock ticked loudly.

'Do you think she's warm enough?' Carly asked.

Her father nodded. 'And I've just changed her drip. This new one should last through the night.' He checked to see that they had resuscitation equipment on hand, just in case.

'She stood back to give him room. 'Why are they called Norwegian Forest cats?' she wanted to know.

'Because that's where the breed originally came from.' Paul rolled the stand for the heavy oxygen cylinder into place. 'The snowy mountains and forests of Scandinavia. See her double coat? That's to keep out the wind and snow. It's quick-drying, too.'

'How come?' Carly watched the cat lick her

lips and try to raise her head. But she was too weak, and she soon sank back.

'The guard hairs are water-resistant. They're covered in oil, so it's as if she's wearing a water-proof jacket.'

'That's amazing. Something to keep out the wind and snow.'

'You want to know another strange thing about this breed?'

'Yes, please.' Carly felt more confident seeing the oxygen mask and trachea tube. If anything did go wrong during the night, they would be ready.

'When they come down from a tree, they come head first, round and round the trunk in a spiral.'

'Huh! I love her long nose and ears. And look at her paws; they're really wide.'

'Yes, she's a nice cat,' Paul agreed. He joined Carly to gaze into the unit.

'Don't say it like that,' she murmured.

'Like what?'

'Like you're sad because you don't think she'll make it.' Like Jordan, she longed to believe that Bubble would survive.

'She's been in a collision with a motor-bike,' Paul reminded her. 'The shock alone could be enough to kill her.' He turned and flicked off the main light, leaving the room in semi-darkness. 'We'll just have to wait and see.

At eight, and then again at nine o'clock that night, Carly left the flat where she and her dad were watching TV to check on Bubble. She saw the cat lying peacefully, eyes closed, with the steady rise and fall of the greenish-coloured line showing clearly on the screen beside her. All was well. She went back to the sofa and piled the cushions around her, flicked channels, then settled in for her favourite comedy programme.

Her dad brought her a hot chocolate drink, then went off to his room to strum a tune on his guitar. It was at quiet times like this, Carly knew, that her dad most missed her mum, who had died suddenly when Carly was four years old. The family had been living and working in Africa. Carly's mum had been Kenyan Asian; it was from her that she'd inherited her brown eyes and jet-black hair. But her hair had her dad's wave in it.

After her mum had died, Paul had brought Carly back to live in England. On a shelf beside his bed he kept a picture of the three of them together; him standing with his hands on Carly's mum's shoulders, Carly curled up on her mum's knee.

'Telly off!' he called from his room, as the theme music played at the end of the programme. 'Time for bed!' Carly yawned and stretched. 'Can I just go and check Bubble one more time?'

'If you're quick.'

So she went in stockinged feet, padding downstairs, across reception and up to intensive care, expecting to see the rhythmic rise and fall of the heartbeat monitor, to hear the tiny blip that showed the cat's condition was stable.

She opened the door and peered into the darkened room. '*Blip . . . blip . . . blip . . . blip.*' The machine told Carly that Bubble's pulse held steady.

Or did it? Wasn't the sound more uneven? She crept forward to look at the screen. The line jumped and skipped, then shot into jagged peaks. Then it strung out on a continuous level. *'Blee-eep!'* It sounded its high warning tone.

Crash! Carly knew what that meant. The cat's heart had stopped beating. If she didn't act quickly they would lose her.

She ran to the phone on the wall and buzzed the flat. 'Dad, come quick! Bubble's heart has stopped!'

Now what? She dashed to the unit to check she wasn't mistaken. No, the monitor showed no sign of a heartbeat. What would her dad do next? Unhook the oxygen mask, put it over the cat's face, turn on the gas. She was all thumbs as she hurried to do it.

But how much oxygen should Carly give her? Should she wait? What else could she do to try to save the patient?

On the wall the clock ticked. A second seemed like an age as she waited for Paul to arrive. Beneath the mask Bubble lay lifeless.

'It's OK, I'll take over!' Paul dashed in and took in what Carly had already done. 'Good girl!' He turned on the gas supply and asked her to hold the mask in place while he listened with a stethoscope to the cat's chest.

He shook his head. 'Nothing.'

Carly's eyes were fixed on the blank screen. Still the seconds ticked on.

'OK, I'm going to massage the chest,' he decided, turning the cat on to her back and telling Carly to take the mask and keep the head turned to the side. Then he leaned on the chest with both his palms, pressing firmly to push air out of the lungs. 'Breathe!' he muttered.

'Nothing!' Carly glanced up at the monitor.

'Let's try again.' Her dad repeated the procedure, pressing down with a low, impatient grunt.

'Again!' she pleaded.

'No, we need more oxygen. Put the mask back on.' He was going to try something else. A last desperate measure to revive the unconscious cat. 'If I'm right, the lungs haven't been working well enough to supply the heart with oxygenated blood. So the heart can't pump. What we have to do is clear whatever's stopping the lungs from taking in air. It's probably blood and fluid from an internal wound.'

He spoke rapidly, reaching for a gleaming scalpel. 'Can you manage to hold the mask?' he asked.

'I think so.' Carly nodded. She gritted her teeth and concentrated on her own task.

Within seconds, Paul performed the surgery needed if they were to save Bubble's life. He made an incision between two ribs and inserted a suction tube into the lung cavity. Soon he was drawing out the fluid that had caused the problem. 'That's better. This should give her a chance to breathe on her own.'

He turned up the oxygen supply from the tank.

Carly watched the cat's ribcage rise as the lungs filled with air. Then they fell and rose again. 'Yes!' She let go of her own held breath and gazed down at the still-unconscious patient.

'Look!' Her dad pointed at the screen. The thin green line blipped up . . . down . . . up, growing stronger, more regular. He waited until the heartbeat was clearly back on the monitor, then checked the cat's pulse.

'Did we do it, Dad?' Carly could hardly believe what the machine was telling them.

He put his finger on the inside of the cat's thigh and counted. Then he nodded. 'Thanks to you,' he told her. 'If you hadn't come in just as Bubble was crashing, she wouldn't have stood a chance!'

Next morning Paul Grey rang the Smiths in Church Street to give them the good news that Bubble had made it through the night.

'We did have a bit of a crisis,' he admitted, 'but we got to the bottom of the problem, fingers crossed.' He looked up at Carly as she passed through reception. 'Bubble's breathing well now. We've taken her off the drip and she seems quite comfortable. Tell Jordan he can come and see her whenever he wants.'

Carly paused by the door until he came off the phone. 'Is it OK if I go to meet Hoody?' she asked, hoping that he wouldn't need her help during morning surgery.

'Sure. We haven't got much booked in and Mel's coming in to do some overtime, so I guess we can manage without you!'

So she slipped out before the queues started to form and made for City Road, her head still full of monitors, masks and all the life-saving equipment they'd used when Bubble had crashed.

After the emergency of the night before, meeting up at the church seemed a bit tame, she had to admit. In a way, she would have liked to have stayed at Beech Hill to see Jordan Smith's face when his parents brought him to visit his cat. Still, she'd promised Hoody. She turned into Church Street, deep in thought.

'Hi.' He stepped out of a shop doorway right in front of her.

'Hoody, you made me jump!'

'That was the idea.'

'Where's Vinny?' She looked round for his friendly dog.

'At home. We're supposed to be following cats, aren't we? Vinny would only chase them.' Hoody led her halfway across the road to a traffic island. On the corner of the main road was a pub called the Hare and Hounds, and beside it, set well back behind its crooked rows of gravestones, stood the disused church.

Carly caught up with Hoody on the island. 'Come on, the road's clear.' What was he waiting for?

'So where are all these cats Mel was on about?' he demanded, joining her by the churchyard wall. He looked tense and pale, turning up his collar and scowling up and down the street.

She stood on tiptoe and peered over the wall. 'I don't know. I can't see anything for grass and nettles.' They would have to go in and make a proper search. Carly tried the rusty iron gates leading up a flagged path into the dark church porch. 'Locked,' she told him. 'We'll have to climb over.'

'Why don't we wait here?' he suggested. 'Until a cat comes along. Then we could follow it.'

'We could wait all day, that's why.' What was wrong with him today? 'All we have to do is climb over the wall and have a good scout around, looking for signs of what the cats are after when they cross the road.' She made it sound simple.

'Actually into the graveyard?' He peered over her shoulder at the stone crosses and sooty angels.

41

'Why not? There's no one around to stop us.' The whole place was deserted. The church's arched windows were boarded up and there wasn't a soul in sight.

'There's dead bodies in there,' Hoody objected, drawing back from the overgrown tangle.

'We won't step on the graves, if that's what's worrying you.'

He shuddered, looking for another excuse not to follow Carly as she hitched herself on to the wall. 'There's a house at the back of this church-yard, you know!'

Carly remembered an old place where the priest had lived when the church was still in use. 'But there's no one there now!'

'How do we know that?' Gritting his teeth, not wanting to be left behind, he hauled himself on to the wall and stared down at the graves.

'Because the priest would have had to leave when they closed the church.' For some reason, the cold wind rustled through the grass and Hoody's jumpiness had begun to spook her too. So she snapped at him and jumped quickly to the ground. She landed between two stone

42

crosses in the middle of a bed of nettles. 'Ouch!' Her hand stung where it had brushed the tips of the leaves.

'Are you sure about this?' Reluctantly Hoody joined her. He stared round the silent graves as if he expected a ghost to jump out.

'This is why you wanted me to meet you, isn't it?' Carly demanded.

'No!' He defended himself and, to show that the place didn't bother him, he stepped ahead between two rows of mouldering graves. But something rustled in the grass and he stopped dead. 'What was that?'

Carly saw a black shadow creep out from behind a gravestone. It went on all fours, silently, stealthily. 'It's only a cat!' she breathed.

Hoody blew through his cheeks. The black cat turned its green eyes on them, then decided to ignore them. It prowled on towards the church door.

From inside the old building came a faint knocking noise, a steady clatter of wood against wood. Once more, Hoody stopped and stared at Carly.

'It's probably only a door banging in a draught,' she whispered. She steadied herself against a gravestone as the cat crept on towards the porch, then at the last minute veered off round the side of the church. 'That's funny.'

'I'm not laughing!' Hoody swallowed hard. 'It's creepy!'

'Come on, let's follow it!' If they dithered much longer, worrying about the graves, they would lose the cat. She crossed the yard and found an overgrown path, climbed a rusting iron fence and found herself round the back of the church, facing yet more crumbling old graves shaped like stone tables and, beyond them, a tall, old-fashioned house.

Behind her, Hoody struggled over the fence. 'Where's it gone? Can you see it?'

She pointed to a shadowy shape stalking across the flat tops of the graves. It jumped from one to another with graceful ease, tail held high, green eyes glittering. 'It it's mice it's looking for, it's decided there's nothing worth bothering about inside the church!' It was definitely heading for the house where the priest had lived.

'Look!' Hoody pointed to a second cat sitting on the low slate roof of an outhouse that joined on to the main building.

The black-and-white tom stared back at them unconcerned.

'And behind us!' Carly turned to see a third cat crossing the graves. By now, the first black cat had reached the edge of the churchyard. It gave a loud miaow and, with one big, agile leap, joined the black-and-white cat on the roof. 'They're all over the place!'

'This is really giving me the creeps!' Hoody shook his head, ready to turn back. 'They can't be hunting mice. They're making too much racket.'

'So, what are they doing here?' Carly stared at the empty house. Old autumn leaves had drifted against the step, up to the faded, peeling wooden door. The walls had ivy growing up to the roof, and broken windows. Old, grey curtains blew in the wind.

'I don't know and I don't care!' Hoody caught her arm. 'Come on, Carly, let's get out of here!'

'Ssh! Didn't you hear something?' She pulled

away, took a step forward. The three cats set up a chorus of wailing calls.

'Yes, cats!' Hoody looked wildly over his shoulder. 'Here comes another one!'

'No, not them. Something else!' She held up her hand and tried to make him listen. 'Footsteps!'

'You must be joking!' Hoody looked for the nearest way out.

But it was too late. It was Carly's turn to grab him. She held him tight as the hollow footsteps from inside the house stopped, a metal bolt was drawn back, and slowly, with an eerie creak, the ancient door opened.

4

An old woman reached out a skinny hand and put a large metal dish on the top step. She peered across the graveyard, head poking forward, her other hand clutching a woollen scarf to her scrawny neck. Her shoulders were hunched, her hair grey and wispy.

'Carly, let's go!' Hoody panicked.

'Shh!' She stood her ground. The old woman seemed short-sighted. As long as they used the gravestones to hide behind and kept dead still, she probably wouldn't spot them.

Stooping to rattle the dish, the woman called out in a thin, cracked voice, 'Here, kitty, kitty, kitty!'

The sleek black cat slung to the edge of the outhouse roof and leaped down. The tom followed more clumsily. They padded towards the dish, tails flicking eagerly.

The old woman saw them and disappeared inside the dark house. As the two cats began to feed from the dish, she came back with a second and then a third, groaning as she stooped, and muttering aloud about her aches and pains.

Meanwhile, half a dozen more cats appeared out of nowhere: grey, ginger and white, big and small, fat and thin, stealing out of the shadows of the church, or across the yard at the back of the Hare and Hounds, over the wall into the overgrown garden of the old house. They came silently up the stone steps and jostled for position at the brimming feeding bowls, heads down, snapping at the meat with their pointed teeth.

'There, that's all you're getting today. You must think I'm made of money! Tut-tut, greedy things!'

The old woman grumbled, but she sounded pleased to see the gang of cats crowding round. 'There, you'd better leave some for Mr T, or he'll be cross!'

'Mr T?' Hoody's jaw had dropped in surprise as once more the weird old woman disappeared inside the house.

'Never mind that. Don't you see what's happening?' Carly leaned out from behind a stone cross to get a better view. 'She's the one who's tempting all the cats to cross the main road – with all the food she puts out!'

Still more cats came surging through the long grass, ignoring Carly and Hoody in their rush to get at the food. Soon there were more than a dozen crowded round the dishes on the step.

'But who's this Mr T?' Hoody almost forgot his fear of graveyards in his curiosity to work out exactly what was going on. He came out from behind a stone ledge and stood on top of a slab carved with a dead man's name.

'Watch it, Hoody!' Carly saw the moss-covered slab rock under his weight. She had one eye on the hungry cats at the open door and one eye on him as he tipped forward, then struggled to get his balance.

'Oh-o-oh!' he yelled, his arms flailing wildly. He slid down the tilting slab, jumped clear and rolled in the grass.

The slab rocked back with an echoing thud. Carly's taut nerves snapped. She screamed.

'Who's there?' The old woman's sharp voice called as she hobbled back to the door. The cats swarmed round her feet, she grasped the door-post with a gnarled hand and peered out once more. 'It's no use hiding, I know there's some-one out there!' she shrilled.

Hoody rolled and jumped up. 'I'm out of here!' he cried. He legged it back the way they'd come, through a gap in the iron fence, across the grave-yard to Church Street.

'Hoody, wait!' Carly took a last look at the doorway. The old woman's voice had risen to a witch-like cackle. The cats ignored the row and shoved forward for the last scraps. She turned and saw Hoody scramble over the far wall. 'Come back!'

Too late; he was gone. She decided to follow,

dodging back between the graves, her head full of unanswered questions.

'Who *was* that?' Hoody stood out of breath on the corner of City Road and Church Street. He'd taken refuge in the doorway of the pub, out of the way of early shoppers.

'How should I know? I never got the chance to find out,' Carly said pointedly. It was time to regroup, to decide on their next move.

'No, and it wasn't you who nearly fell into a pile of old bones either!' he reminded her of his narrow escape.

'OK, but if we'd kept quiet and stuck around, we might have found out more.' Carly sat on the step to catch her breath. 'Like, what's that old woman doing there in the first place? I thought the whole house was empty, along with the church!'

'Fancy living in that wreck!' Hoody couldn't imagine it. 'Spooky!'

'And does she live by herself? And why is she feeding all the neighbourhood cats? Doesn't she realise that most of them are risking their nine lives every time they cross the road to get to the food? Hasn't she got the sense to see that?' Her voice rose in anger as she remembered what had happened to Bubble.

'Calm down.' Hoody sat beside her, his elbows resting on his knees. 'Let's just both take it easy, OK?'

'That's easy for you to say.' But she stopped and took a deep breath. 'The thing is, Hoody, that old woman's actually killing cats with kindness!'

'I know.' He hung his head and stared at the pavement.

Just then, the door behind them opened and the landlord of the Hare and Hounds almost tripped over their hunched figures. 'I thought so!' he muttered as he stopped to collar Carly. 'Aren't you the two I just saw messing about in the churchyard?'

'We weren't doing anything wrong,' she protested.

Hoody jumped up and spun round, ready for an argument.

'So you call trespassing not doing anything wrong, do you?' The burly, middle-aged man stared sarcastically at them. 'And I suppose camping out on my front doorstep is OK too?'

'We're sorry.' Carly was quick to apologise. 'We didn't mean to get in your way.'

Hoody glowered at her for backing down.

But it made the landlord soften his tone. 'Well, I didn't mean to yell at you either. It's just that I'm fed up with kids climbing the wall into that place,' he told them. 'And with all the stray cats that come calling. You should hear them at night, howling away. I just wish the church lot would decide what's going to happen to the land and get on with selling it, then I can get some peace and quiet.'

'Does it happen a lot?' Carly was eager to keep him talking.

'What? The kids or the cats?'

'The cats. How come there's so many?'

'Because it's the main meeting place for every cat in the district, that's why! My flat above the pub overlooks the churchyard, so I see them come and go, day in, day out. I've just about had enough. Personally I can't stand the horrible things!'

53

'Who's the woman that feeds them?' Hoody spoke for the first time. He got straight to the point.

The landlord gave a half-laugh. 'You mean the cat lady? That's what we all call her round here. Don't talk to me about her!'

'Why not?' Hoody insisted.

'She's got a screw loose, that one.' He shook his head. 'Lives there all by herself. Her whole world is cats, cats, cats!'

'But we thought the church was closed.' Carly probed for more information. 'How come she's still there?'

The landlord shrugged. 'Search me. But she's been there as long as anyone round here can remember. She used to be the housekeeper to the priest, who lived there and looked after the Catholics in the parish. They call the house The Presbytery. But don't ask me why they didn't send the old woman packing when they closed the church and moved the priest. It doesn't make any sense to me.'

'Hasn't anyone asked her?' Carly thought it was odd that the landlord was so vague.

'We've tried. I've even gone knocking on her door a couple of times to see if she needs anything. But it's no good. She keeps herself to herself. In fact, last time I called, she leaned out of the window and threatened to set the police on to me!'

'Weird!' Hoody said, ready to believe that the witchy old cat lady was truly off her head.

'Well, there's not much we can do with someone like that, I have to admit.' The landlord sized up both Hoody and Carly. 'And whatever you were doing in that churchyard—'

'We were following—' Carly broke in.

'No, don't tell me. Whatever it was, my advice is to steer well clear in future!'

On the way back to the Rescue Centre, Hoody said the landlord was right. Carly said he was wrong. They had a massive argument.

'How can you say that?' She stood in the carpark at Beech Hill, almost shouting. 'If we don't go back and try to talk that old woman out of feeding the cats, there's going to be another accident on that street any day now!'

'Yeah! Well, what do you suggest? We go sneaking back through those graves and knock on her rotten door? "Excuse me, Cat Lady, but did you know you were a nutty old lady who shouldn't be feeding these little kitties? They're all getting squished on the road because of you!" ' Hoody yelled back. He even ignored his friend, Bob the Old English sheepdog, he was so mad.

'You're only saying that because you're too scared to go in there again!' Even as she said this, Carly wished that she hadn't. She clamped her mouth tight shut and went bright red.

There was a thumping silence. Hoody glared at her. A tiny nerve under his eye flickered as Bob came bounding up. 'Next time you want someone to walk your dogs, don't come asking me, OK!' he yelled. He turned away, not waiting for her to say sorry, cutting across the carpark and out of the gates. He was a skinny, lonely figure disappearing down the hill.

'What was that all about?' A voice broke into Carly's jumble of feelings.

She looked up and recognised Julie Sutton, the

centre's expert in animal behaviour who came in once or twice a week to work with problem dogs. She was an easy-going, middle-aged woman with small round glasses, who always wore the same fawn, zip-up jacket, brown trousers and stout lace-up shoes. 'Cats,' Carly answered, trying to hide the tears that had welled up as Hoody stormed off. 'Nothing. Never mind.'

'Bob, here!' Julie called the large dog to heel – he'd started to race off after Hoody, surprised at being ignored by him. She praised him when he obeyed. 'I promised your dad I'd take this fellow home for a few days and get him knocked into shape,' she told Carly. 'How do you rate my chances?'

'Good.' She nodded and swallowed back her own urge to chase after Hoody and make up. *Give him time to get over it*, she thought.

Julie patted Bob and led him to her car. 'Thanks for that vote of confidence,' she called with a cheery wave.

So Carly went in through the main entrance, glad to see a busy waiting room and a queue of patients to take her mind off Hoody and the cat lady. She met Jordan Smith on his way out with his mum and dad. 'How's Bubble?' she asked.

'Getting better.' Jordan held his dad's hand. 'They did an operation to mend her heart!'

Tina Smith smiled. 'She knows that, Jordan.' As the family passed by, she winked at Carly. 'Thanks for what you did!' she whispered.

'They're going to take pictures of her bones!' Jordan went on, his big brown eyes shining. 'They're going to show them to me next time I come to visit!'

Carly smiled back, then carried on through reception, changing her outdoors jacket for a green plastic apron and hurrying through to the X-ray room to see how the Smiths' cat was doing.

She found Liz and her dad studying the X-rays on a special screen, while Mel helped the patient come round from her dose of anaesthetic. 'Here you are, just in time!' The nurse wrapped Bubble in a blanket and handed her to Carly.

She took the dazed cat and held her close.

'Don't look so glum. It's good news,' Paul called across. 'The jaw isn't broken, it's just dislocated. We shan't need surgery to correct that. With a bit of luck we'll be able to manipulate it back into place when the swelling and bruising from the accident have gone down.'

'Good. What about the broken rib?' Carly asked.

'That should mend in its own good time. In fact, with good nursing and round-the-clock care for the next forty-eight hours, there's no reason why Bubble shouldn't make a full recovery.'

Carly smiled and took the cat upstairs to the warmth and safety of the intensive care unit. As she popped Bubble carefully back on to the soft blanket lining the plastic cage and released her from her grasp, the cat miaowed. Her rough pink tongue licked Carly's hand.

'Don't worry, Jordan will come and visit you again as soon as he can,' she promised. She knew that sick cats always pined for their owners. She talked as if Bubble understood every word. 'And you'll be out of here and back home before you know it!'

5

'This is when I'm glad I do what I do,' Paul Grey said. It was Sunday morning, the September sun was shining through the blinds, and Carly and he were ready to take Bubble out of intensive care. 'A nice quiet day; no surgery to run, no pressure and a success story in the shape of this pretty little cat!'

He whistled as he wheeled aside the trolley for the heart monitor and oxygen cylinder.

Carefully Carly took Bubble out of the unit. Despite her little patches of shaved fur, she really was beautiful. Her ears were larger, her nose longer than an ordinary cat's, and she had a full ruff of soft, blue-grey fur. But it was her eyes that made her so special and mysterious. They were set wide apart, slanted slightly upwards at the outer corners, and were the most stunning deep amber.

'Let's put her in the cage at the end of the row,' Paul decided. 'She'll be nice and warm there. Put a dish of water in with her. Later today we'll have a go at clicking the jawbone back into place, then we'll see how she tackles her first meal.'

Carly handled the injured cat gently. She made her comfortable on a blanket in her new home and stroked her before she closed the door. She felt her dad study her from a distance, but didn't look up to meet his gaze.

'Would I be right in thinking that you're not your usual chirpy self?' he asked quietly.

'I'm OK, thanks.' She'd rather not talk about what was bothering her until she'd decided what to do next. Should she tackle the problem of Hoody or the cat lady first? Both were hard ones to solve, and she'd lain awake till late the night before thinking about them.

'Where's Hoody this morning?' her dad asked, his head to one side, still piercing her with his gaze.

'I don't know.' On a normal Sunday Hoody would show up with Vinny to take a dog to the park.

Paul ignored her blushes. 'Do I take it you two have had an argument?' Raising a slat on the blind he glanced down into the carpark. 'Uh-oh, talk of the devil. Here he comes now.'

Carly jumped. 'Are you sure?' She ran to the window and looked down. There he was, hands in pockets, ambling up to the door as if nothing had happened.

Without a word, she left her dad to it and took the stairs down into reception two at a time. She reached the door as Hoody arrived and shoved it open.

'Sorry!' she gasped.

'Sorry!' Hoody said in the same split second.

'I didn't mean what I said about you being scared. Anyway, I was really spooked too. Anyone would be!'

'You were right: someone has got to go and talk to the old woman.'

They both stopped and gave a self-conscious grin. That was all it took – a relieved sigh and the row was over.

'I'm gonna walk the dogs,' Hoody said with a shrug. 'Do you want to come?'

One problem solved, one to go, Carly thought as she stood at the park gates and watched her friend walk off with Vinny and two black Labradors from the kennels. The three dogs chased the sticks he threw for them with excited barks, rushing down the slope towards the swings and roundabouts.

Now for the cat lady.

This was the way it had worked out with Hoody. After they'd both said sorry, he'd said he would come back to St Martin's with her if she really wanted him to. But Carly had known he was only being nice and saying it to make up for the day before.

'You don't need to come,' she'd said quietly. 'I don't mind going by myself.'

He'd quickly thought of reasons for letting her. 'Maybe she's more likely to listen if there's just one of us.' And, 'It would probably be a better idea for me to take the dogs to the park while you go back there.'

Carly had said he was right. 'If I was an old lady living by myself, I might be scared to answer the door if there was more than one kid knocking. Yes, it's much better if I go alone.'

She'd sounded braver and more cheerful than she'd felt at the time. And now, as she watched Hoody go off with the dogs, she began to dread doing what they'd agreed on. Nevertheless, she tried to talk sensibly to herself as she crossed Beech Hill and made her way up to City Road.

'What can one old lady do to you?' she demanded. 'She looks like a witch from a fairy-tale. So what? She's supposed to be nutty. *So what*? She likes cats, doesn't she? That means she can't be all bad!'

She walked along City Road with determined steps until she reached the corner of Church Street. There was St Martin's Church with its tall soot-blackened steeple set against the blue sky.

There was the crumbling graveyard with its long grass and nettles, the crooked ancient grave-stones.

The hairs on Carly's neck began to prickle when she saw them. 'Here lieth James Heath and his wife, Jane, who departed this life on the second of March 1746. In their deaths they were not divided.' She read the inscription on a head-stone near the locked gate and shivered. What disaster had befallen James and his wife? And 'Here lies Maria, daughter of Thomas and Eliza Moore, born and died 1st of August, 1837. Suffer little children to come unto me.'

Quickly, before her nerve gave way, Carly jumped over the wall and ran between the graves.

' "All things bright and beautiful,

All creatures great and small . . ." '

At the sound of the high, cracked voice singing the hymn, Carly stopped. She dodged behind the church wall and peered out at the old priest's house.

' "All things wise and wonderful . . ." Here, kitty, kitty, kitty!' A metal dish rattled against the doorstep as a skinny hand set it down.

Carly saw half a dozen eager cats scurry down slate roofs, between gravestones, across the overgrown garden. They pushed and jostled for position at the brimming feeding bowls.

' "The Lord God made them all." ' The old lady looked up and saw Carly watching her. She drew up one hand to clutch the scarf at her throat. 'Go away!' she shrieked. 'Or I'll call the police!'

'No, it's OK, I only wanted to talk to you.' Carly gathered her courage and stepped forward, down some mossy steps leading from the churchyard into the presbytery garden.

'People are always pestering us. Do we need this? Do we need that? Why don't they leave us alone? Go on, go away! I don't want to talk to you! Shoo!' Waving her gnarled hands to make Carly back off, she stepped inside the dark house and began to close the door. 'Whatever you've come for, I don't want to listen!'

'It's about the cats!' Carly pleaded in a loud voice.

The door stopped closing, the old woman peered out. 'Cats, you say?'

'Yes. I'm Carly Grey. I live at Beech Hill Rescue Centre.'

'No need to shout.' The old woman came out grumbling. 'I may be old but I'm not deaf.'

'I'm sorry . . .'

'What about my kitties?' She gazed fondly at the swarm of cats feeding at her feet. Latecomers from Church Street were still crossing the church-yard and speeding past Carly to get at the bowls of food.

Slowly Carly approached along the weed-choked path. She noticed that though some of the cats wore collars and looked well-fed, others were thin and scraggy with dull coats. One had only half a tail, another had a torn ear. 'Which ones belong to you?' she asked as she drew near. The old lady had definitely said 'my kitties'.

'All, all!' the old lady cried. 'We're all God's creatures! The Lord God made us all!'

'But which ones are actually yours?' Carly kept her talking. Close to, she could see that the cat lady's thin face was criss-crossed with tiny, dry lines, but that her grey eyes were still bright. 'Does that one with only half a tail live here?'

The tough young tabby cat was scrapping with his neighbour for the last mouthfuls of food.

'Live here? On my goodness, no!' The old lady opened her mouth and laughed. 'Mr T wouldn't like that one little bit!'

'Who's Mr T?' *That name again*. Carly imagined a tiny frail old husband for the cat lady. He was probably laid up with arthritis, too old to mend the house and keep it in good order, too ill even to go out. And it sounded as if he didn't like cats!

'Mr T may not get out much these days,' the old lady seemed to pick up Carly's thoughts, 'but he'd definitely have something to say if I adopted young Half-Tail there!' She glanced shrewdly at Carly. 'Aren't you the same dark-haired girl who came here with the tall boy yesterday?'

Carly swallowed hard. 'Did you see us?'

'I heard you first of all, then I saw you run off, clear as day. I may be old, but I'm not blind!' Her eyes creased and disappeared behind layers of wrinkles. She gave a cackling laugh.

'I'm sorry if we scared you.'

Another laugh. 'That's funny; I seem to re-member it was the other way around! I've never seen two people move so fast as you and that young boy.'

Carly gave a nervous grin back. 'You made us jump. We didn't expect anyone to be still living here.' She glanced up at the ivy-covered walls and peeling paintwork.

The old lady nodded and sighed. 'I know. Nothing's been done to the old house for years, not since the bishop decided the church was to close and all the parishioners were to start going to services at the new church at Fiveways. And we wouldn't still be here except for Mr T. You can blame him for that.'

Turning back to the cats, who were quietly grooming themselves in the sun, she sighed again and began to hum the hymn tune once more.

Piece by piece Carly slotted the puzzle into place: the church had closed and the priest had moved on to a new parish. By rights the house-keeper should have moved too. But the bishop had let her and her husband stay on. 'Don't you have anywhere else to go?' Instead of being scared, she was beginning to feel sorry for the old lady and her frail, housebound husband.

The housekeeper tutted. 'There's my daughter, Christine, in Putney for a start. And I've a sister in Birmingham. No, the real problem is that it wouldn't be fair to expect Mr T to move at his time of life.'

Carly nodded sympathetically. She was about to move on and gently explain how the cat lady's kindness to her 'kitties' was actually putting them in danger.

'Would you like to come in and meet him?' she went on, to Carly's surprise. Without waiting for an answer, she led the way inside the house.

So Carly had no choice but to follow down a dark corridor with panelled doors off to left and right. The cream wallpaper was faded and damp and a bare electric bulb cast a gloomy light.

'He's in the kitchen,' the old lady croaked. 'I expect we'll find him in his favourite chair as usual.'

As she opened the door, Carly thought she could smell fish. She glimpsed an old-fashioned gas cooker and a wickerwork rocking chair with its back to the door.

'That's Mr T's breakfast you can smell.' She held the door and waited for Carly. 'He won't eat anything except the very best. He's getting fussy in his old age.' With her slow, stooped walk, she edged forward and beckoned Carly into the room. 'And of course he's a bit deaf, and his eyesight isn't what it used to be, is it, Mr T?'

Carly prepared herself for a polite hello. She cleared her throat and moved round to the front of the big round-backed chair. 'Oh!'

'What's the matter?' The old lady was puzzled by Carly's open-mouthed stare. 'I thought you liked cats.'

'I – I do!' There on a faded patchwork cushion, blinking sleepily at her, was a fat ginger tom.

'Well, meet Mr T. He's seventeen years old, and though he's a bit stiff and creaky he's still my very own pride and joy!'

Mr T was a grand old cat with striped orange fur and a white chest. His whiskery face was marked from battles fought long ago. There was a small chunk bitten out of his ear, an old scar across his pink nose. He purred as Carly stroked him.

'Like I said, he can't get about much.' The old lady had introduced Mr T, then told Carly her own name: Lily Andrews. She'd boiled a kettle on the old hob and made them both a cup of tea. 'He has rheumatics, poor old thing.' She leaned forward with Carly's cup and whispered privately. 'He doesn't like us to talk about his ailments; it makes him feel old!'

'Why don't you bring him to Beech Hill?' Carly asked. 'My dad could take a look at him and see if there's anything he could do to help.'

'Oh no, no vets!' Lily's mouth set in a firm, thin line. 'I don't hold with vets unless there's an emergency. No, with Mr T it's old age pure and simple.'

The cat opened his mouth wide and yawned.

'He's not unhappy,' the old lady insisted. It just means I have to look after him more than I used to.' She took a white saucer with sprigs of roses round the rim and began to spoon the cooked fish into it. 'I always give him his food in his favourite dish and put it in the same corner of the room so he knows exactly where to find it. And I leave the furniture in the same place so he doesn't bump into things.'

Carly watched Mr T stand up and stretch. Groggily he got down from the chair and hobbled over to the saucer.

'Of course, he wouldn't cope if we had to move to a new home. The bishop was very good about it when I explained why I would like to stay on in the old house. He understands the way I feel about Mr T. Since I lost my husband, Mr T has been my best friend.' She stood back, arms folded, watching him munch steadily. 'Round here they call me the cat lady!' she said proudly.

'I know that.' Carly seized her chance to broach the subject she'd come to talk about. 'It must cost you a lot of money to keep on feeding all the neighbourhood cats.'

'Oh, I don't mind that. There's only me to look after beside the cats, and I don't have to pay the church any rent while I live here.' She glanced shrewdly at Carly. 'Half of them are strays living in the old churchyard. They would starve to death if I didn't feed them.'

'But the others have already got owners. They get plenty to eat at home.'

Mrs Andrews tutted. 'What's the harm in spoiling them with an extra treat once in a while?' She waited until Mr T had finished the fish, then put down a matching saucer of milk.

'Well, that's just it.' Carly jumped in with both feet. 'They're the ones who have to cross Church Street to get here. And that's a busy road. There have been a few accidents—'

'Nonsense!' the old lady cut in sharply. 'I'd have known about it if any of my cats got run over.'

'But just last Friday one of them *was*: Bubble, a long-haired grey cat . . . A motor-bike crashed into her when she was crossing the road to get here.'

'No!' She waved her hand impatiently and led Carly down the corridor to the front dor. Her mood had changed the minute Carly had tried to explain.

'Mrs Andrews, listen for a moment!' Carly grew desperate to make her understand. 'Couldn't you stop putting food out? I know you mean to be kind, but it really is dangerous!' Already she was out on the step, looking back at the cat lady.

'And turn them away when they come to my door crying for food?' She shook her head. 'I couldn't do that. I wouldn't have the heart.'

'But Bubble nearly died!' Carly put out a hand to stop Mrs Andrews from shutting the door. 'There's bound to be another accident before long if you go on feeding them!'

The door closed. Carly stared at its cracked and peeling surface. She leaned forward and put her ear against it, wondering what the old lady would do now. From inside the house she heard the old tune: ' "All things bright and beautiful . . . All creatures great and small . . ." '

From the sunny outhouse roof, three cats stared down at her.

' "Each little flower that opens . . . Each little bird that sings . . ." '

It was hopeless. Mrs Andrews hadn't listened to a word Carly had said.

6

'How *does* she do that?' Hoody asked. He and Carly sat on the swings in the park watching Julie Sutton put Bob through his paces, while Vinny lay quietly taking a nap.

The Old English sheepdog was unrecognisable from the noisy, disobedient creature Julie had taken home with her only days earlier. He sat when she ordered him to sit, stayed to heel, ran to fetch a stick at her command.

'I don't know. It's brilliant!' Carly wanted to clap as Bob trotted back and dropped the stick at the trainer's feet. He sat neatly, huge feet together, looking up and waiting for his reward. Julie gave him a pat on the head and a smart 'Good boy. Well done.'

'She doesn't even have to bribe him with treats,' Hoody pointed out.

'Stay!' Julie held up a warning finger and made the dog sit where he was as she came across to the swings. 'What do you think?' She asked for their verdict, her round face wreathed in smiles.

'Amazing! I'd never have believed it.' Carly remembered the problems they'd had with Bob before, when a walk to the park meant strained arm sockets as the giant dog towed them along.

'Cool.' For Hoody, this was high praise. 'How do you do it?'

Julie sat on the next swing. 'Here, Bob!'

He sprang up and raced across the grass.

'Sit!' Julie hooked her arm up sharply, bending it at the elbow; the signal for Bob to obey.

He sat and gazed eagerly at her from behind his mop of white and grey hair.

'Good boy. Now lie down.' She nodded as he did as he was told. Then she answered Hoody's question. 'It's a matter of letting them know who's boss, that's all. Firm handling, giving them clear instructions, being consistent.'

'Meaning what?' He kept a wary eye on the dogs as Vinny woke from his nap and came to investigate.

'Well, always giving exactly the same set of orders, so they learn to recognise the word and the signal that goes with it.' Julie enjoyed explaining her work to anyone who was interested. 'You must have done that with Vinny yourself to have got him into good shape like you have.'

Hoody ducked his head, pleased by the praise. 'But Vinny was nowhere near so tough to handle in the first place. What made Bob such an idiot?'

'Never blame the dog, blame the owner,' Julie insisted. She took a tough line. 'If owners can't train animals to follow commands, they don't deserve to keep them. I've seen too many confused, mistreated dogs in my time to have any sympathy for the people who've caused the problem. Carly's probably seen the results of bad owners at Beech Hill plenty of times.'

Carly nodded. 'They dump their dogs on us

when they can't be bothered with them any more. Like Bob. It happens often.' The conversation with Julie was making her think.

'You reckon you could train any dog?' Hoody challenged Julie.

'Pretty well. Unless it's been so badly handled, beaten and starved and so on, that it's completely lost its trust of human beings. But mostly a dog wants to be trained.'

'How come?'

'Dogs are pack animals in the wild. Like wolves. That means they're subservient – by instinct they need a leader to follow. When you're training a dog, as long as you're firm and you reward it with praise, you become that leader.'

'Cool.' Hoody liked the idea. He swung forward and jumped off. 'What's your job called?'

Julie too stood up. She took Bob's lead from her pocket. 'I'm an animal behaviourist, to give me my proper title.'

As they called Bob and Vinny to come out of the park, and walked, still chatting about Julie's job, up the slope to the gates, Carly was turning over a new idea. It was Wednesday; three days since she'd come away from St Martin's Church. Packed days of school, helping out at surgery, nursing Bubble back to health. The cat was on the mend: Paul had fixed her dislocated jaw and she was able to eat small amounts of food. In a few days she would be well enough to go home. But meanwhile Carly was no nearer to solving the problem of the cat lady.

'What about cats?' she asked now, seemingly out of the blue.

'Do you mean, do I work with cats?' Julie told Bob to sit at the kerb as they said goodbye to Vinny and Hoody and turned towards the Rescue Centre.

'Yes. Can you train a cat like you can train a dog?'

'In some ways, yes. Cats do have common behaviour problems, such as soiling the carpet, for instance. You can train them to use a cat litter tray, because by nature they're very clean animals.' Julie glanced at Carly. 'That's not what you're getting at, though, is it?'

'No.' Carly had just seen how obedient Bob

had been at the kerbside, and now she was thinking about Bubble.

'Could you teach one not to cross a road?'

'Ah! No, definitely not. To teach a cat road sense would take more magic than I have at my fingertips, I'm afraid.' She shook her head as she went on to explain. 'It goes back to what I said about dogs. Cats aren't pack animals, you see. In the wild they hunt alone, they fight for territory, and they definitely don't like to be led.'

Carly realised Julie was right. 'But you'd think a cat would be clever enough to stay away from a busy road without being taught.'

They turned into the Rescue Centre and Julie was ready to hand Bob back to Liz Hutchins, the assistant vet, who'd spotted them from inside the building.

'And you'd think a human being would be careful enough not to run a cat over with a lethal machine!' she retorted.

'Have we got an owner lined up for Bob yet?' Carly asked Liz as they made him comfortable in his kennel. They had to speak above the noise of a dozen dogs all yapping and barking for attention from the neighbouring kennels.

'A possible. Someone rang up yesterday asking for this breed and was glad when I said her luck might be in. But we haven't met her yet to see if she's going to be suitable.' At Beech Hill they always vetted the people who wanted to adopt an animal. 'She might be the sort who falls in love with the dog on the paint adverts on telly but doesn't know the first thing about actually owning one.'

They moved on down the row, saying hello to each dog. When they came to the last one, Liz opened the door. 'At least Bob has a better chance of finding a suitable owner than poor old Molly here.'

An overweight springer spaniel stared up at them from drooping, bloodshot eyes. She was so heavy she could hardly lift herself and waddle out into the exercise yard after Liz and Carly.

'Twelve years old with a kidney problem.' Liz shook her head sadly. 'The family who owned her couldn't cope with her weeing all over the place so they gave her to us.'

She crouched to pat and make a fuss of the dog. 'Old age; it's not to be recommended, is it, Molly?'

'Isn't there anything we can do?' Carly frowned.

'Yes, but her owners didn't want to fork out any money on veterinary care. We can certainly help with the kidneys, and with the rheumatism and the weight problem. Who knows, Molly might have a decent quality of life for another couple of years, given the proper care.'

'Really?' Carly perked up. 'You mean there are drugs to cure old age?'

'Not cure exactly.' Liz let the spaniel waddle back into her kennel and flop down exhausted. 'There's no magic formula, but I have seen dogs who've been on their last legs make surprising progress with the right treatment.'

'What about cats?' The same question that she'd asked Julie Sutton flew out again. But this time Carly was thinking not about Bubble, but about Mr T.

'Yep.' Liz nodded. 'Why do you ask?'

Carly's eyes lit up. 'Tell me how!'

Liz reeled off a list of possibilities. 'If the cat's turning senile in old age, we can prescribe sulphadiazine to combat lack of interest and vitality. Often an old cat refuses to move from his favourite chair, can't be bothered to groom himself or eat properly.'

'Yes!' Carly nodded. This fitted Mr T exactly. 'What else?'

'We can give anabolic hormones to promote tissue building, like athletes who want to put on muscle illegally. It also helps the healing process and increases appetite. Big words, but in effect we're giving the old cat a new lease of life.'

Eagerly Carly pictured it: Mr T back on his feet, no longer an invalid; Mrs Andrews relieved and grateful for all they'd done. She wouldn't need to worry about taking Mr T to a nice new home. She would be able to move out of the crumbling old presbytery to live with her daughter or her sister . . .

'Carly?' Liz clicked her fingers in front of her face. 'Is anyone home?'

'Sorry, yes . . . I was thinking . . .' She stumbled out of the kennels into the corridor. 'Liz . . .'

'What?'

'Are you busy?'

'Yep. Why?' The young vet hurried on ahead.

'*Very* busy?'

'No busier than usual.' She arranged files on Bupinda's desk, filled in forms from evening surgery, checked the clock on the wall which said seven-thirty.

'Are you doing anything this evening?'

'Yes, putting my feet up in front of the telly.' Firmly sliding the files into a drawer and taking off her white coat, Liz turned and confronted Carly. 'Come on, spit it out. You want me to come and see a new patient, don't you?'

Carly held her breath and nodded.

'It's some ancient, deaf and blind cat with rheumatism, isn't it?'

She stared and nodded.

'And the owner can't pay for treatment. It's an old lady living by herself with only her cat for company?'

'How did you guess?'

Liz laughed. 'Easy. I know you better than you think, Carly Grey. And there's no need to look at me with those big brown eyes. The answer's yes, so just get a move on and lead the way!'

For once the churchyard at St Martin's wasn't overrun with cats when Carly and Liz arrived. There was a nip of autumn in the air, rain-clouds hung heavy overhead, and the broken gutters of the old church dripped water on to the soggy earth.

'Charming!' Liz sighed when she saw the presbytery's grimy windows and weed-choked path. 'I wouldn't fancy looking out on to this gloomy view either.' She glanced sideways at the crooked headstones.

Just then a big black crow spread its wings and flew down from the church roof. It squawked as it dived towards them, flapping loudly. Then it veered off across the presbytery garden and rose to perch on the roof there. Inside the house a light went on in a downstairs room, then quickly off again.

'Ready?' Carly led the way across the garden. A second crow flapped low above their heads.

'How on earth did you find out there was

somebody living here?' Liz asked, holding tight to her vet's bag and zipping her jacket. 'No, don't tell me. I don't think I want to know!'

'We followed the cats.' Carly knocked on the door and waited. She had the feeling that Mrs Andrews had already spotted them and didn't want to answer.

'What now?' Liz looked behind at the graves silhouetted against the rainy sky.

Carly knocked again. Then she bent to listen and peek through the letterbox. 'Mrs Andrews?' she called down the dark, dusty hallway.

'Did you hear that?' Liz gripped Carly's arm to draw her away. A high, cracked voice droned along the corridor.

'It's OK, it's only Mrs Andrews singing.' Carly recognised the hymn. She put her mouth to the letterbox and called again. 'Mrs Andrews. It's me: Carly Grey!'

'Go away!' The old lady came to her kitchen door and shrieked down the corridor. 'We don't want to talk to you!'

'We've come to see Mr T!'

'He's not well. We can't have visitors today!'

Liz shook her head. 'Come on, let's go.'

'Wait. I might be able to persuade her.' Carly knew that the old lady cared about one thing only, and that was her cat. 'I've brought someone special to see Mr T!' she called. 'Her name's Liz Hutchins and she's a vet.'

'We don't need a vet, thank you!' came the short reply. But the voice wavered.

'It won't cost you anything. And if Mr T's poorly, she might be able to help.

'He's a bit off-colour, that's all. He's off his food. I can take perfectly good care of him myself.' Mrs Andrews grumbled and tried to convince herself that she didn't need help. Nevertheless she shuffled towards the door. At last she opened it and her pinched, lined face peered out. 'You'd better come in,' she said quietly.

So they followed her slowly into the kitchen, where the window was steamy and a pan of fish boiled on the hob. They found Mr T huddled in his special chair, his front paws tucked under, his head sunk low, eyes dull.

'Hmm.' Liz put down her bag and unzipped her jacket, forgetting any doubts she might have had. 'You're right, he does look a bit off-colour. How long since he ate anything?'

'Monday teatime. Since then he's just picked every now and then. It's not like Mr T; he usually tucks in and licks his plate clean.' Mrs Andrews stood trembling behind the cat's chair, watching anxiously as Liz gently examined the ginger tom. 'I told him it's nothing serious, just a tummy bug. He'll soon be right as rain!' She forced herself to sound brave for Mr T's benefit.

Liz nodded. 'It's not unusual for an elderly cat to lose his appetite.' She eased his mouth open. 'Here's one reason,' she told Carly, inviting her to take a look. There's a build-up of tartar on his teeth and that's caused some damage to his gums. They're bleeding slightly, see?'

Next she took a small torch from her bag and shone it into the cat's ears and eyes Then she listened to his heart with a stethoscope. 'Not bad,' she commented, standing up. 'As far as I can see, there isn't anything specific wrong with him, other than the normal wear and tear of old age.'

'Shh!' The cat lady beckoned Liz across the room into the corridor.

'She doesn't want Mr T to hear you talking about him!' Carly grinned. 'You go. I'll stay here.' She crouched down beside the chair and softly stroked the cat as Liz delivered her diagnosis.

'. . . No magic potions, but we do have some compounds than can help . . . clean up his teeth and get his appetite back . . . become more alert . . . build up his strength . . . I'd say that Mr T is definitely suitable for this kind of treatment.'

Carly and Mr T overheard, despite the old lady's precautions. 'Hear that?' she whispered to him. 'Liz has got some nice medicine for you.'

'Will you have to take him away with you?' Mrs Andrews asked.

'No. We can treat him here at home with tablets. I'll show you how to pop one on to the back of his tongue and make him swallow it down. Then you keep on giving him the medicine yourself. Before you know it, you should be seeing a great improvement in the way he feeds and keeps himself clean.'

'A new lease of life, eh?' The old lady turned the news over in her mind.

'Exactly. Eventually, Mr T will build up

strength and become much more active again.'
Liz sounded calm and confident.

'Did you hear that?' Mrs Andrews poked her
head back into the kitchen. 'No more lazing
about in that chair and having me running
around after you.' She came in smiling, shaking
her head, with tears in her eyes. 'Who would
believe what they can do these days?'

'All being well.' Liz followed and added a
word of caution. She took a small white box of
tablets from her bag. 'One of these twice a day,
with food. And Carly and I will come back in a
couple of days' time to see how Mr T is getting
on.'

7

Thursday was a good day at Beech Hill. The possible owner for Bob, the reformed Old English sheepdog, came in to be vetted by Liz. She was Viv Dearing, a woman of about fifty who had just given up work and lived in a house with a big garden on the edge of town.

'Plenty of time, plenty of space,' Liz noted with approval as Viv took Bob for a trial walk in the park. 'It looks promising.'

As Carly plunged into evening surgery, running along corridors with cat baskets, cleaning down

treatment tables and doubling up as a reception-
ist while Bupinda collected a friend from the
airport, she saw Hoody and Vinny come and go.

'Hey, I've had an idea about the churchyard
cats!' He dropped in a casual sentence as he
swung out of the door with old Molly, the overweight spaniel.

'Aren't you going to tell me?' she called after
him.

'Later.' He was gone, without breaking his
long, loping stride, and without looking back.

'Typical!' Carly lined up the next patient in the
waiting room. But she was too busy to dwell on
it. There was Thumper, a Flemish Giant rabbit
with overgrown incisors, to take for dental treatment into room one. 'He weighs a ton!' she
gasped at her dad as she carried him through.

Then, after surgery, there was the usual feeding
and cleaning out for the resident cats and dogs.
She was upstairs grooming Bubble on a table
with a soft brush when Jordan and his mum came
to visit, and was happy to report that the cat was
making good progress. 'She's starting to take care
of herself again, look,' she pointed out to Jordan.

Bubble was licking her sides with her rough pink tongue, still stiff from the accident, but looking brighter. Carly showed Jordan how to help the cat get the tangles out of her long grey fur. 'You have to straighten it and brush it the way it grows naturally,' she explained.

Jordan took the brush and his mum stood him on a chair so that he could reach the table. Gently he brushed Bubble's thick fur.

'He's been worried to death about that cat,' Tina told Carly. 'It's all he ever talks about. "When will Bubble be better?" "When can she come home?" '

'Soon, I expect.' Carly brought warm water and cotton wool to show them how to clean Bubble's feet and ears. 'Now that she's getting more active, we'll have to make sure she doesn't twist round to pull at her stitches.' She warned them that it could hold Bubble back from getting better if the wound didn't heal properly. 'But don't worry, we'll keep an eye on her.'

Jordan nodded happily and carried on brushing the cat.

'Could I have a word with you?' Tina drew

Carly outside the door. 'It's about the traffic problem outside our house. As you can see, Jordan can't wait to get Bubble back home, but I'm worried about how we'll manage with the cars whizzing up and down as fast as ever. Do you think Bubble will have learned her lesson about busy roads, or is she likely to do the same thing again?'

It was too soon for Carly to let her in on the plan to move Mrs Andrews and Mr T out of the crumbling presbytery. It all depended on whether or not the old cat got better on his course of tablets. 'We hope not,' she told Tina.

'I heard it's all down to some dotty old lady who thinks it's her mission in life to feed every cat around.' Jordan's mother frowned. 'The landlord at the pub told us she's been doing it for months. Well, of course Bubble's going to cross the road if she knows there's a free meal over there every time she looks! And you can't keep a cat inside the house twenty-four hours a day. I don't know what I'm going to do, except that a few of us who own cats are thinking of getting together and going across the road to give the old dear a piece of our minds!'

'Wait for a bit,' Carly said quietly. 'Bubble won't be out of here for a few days yet, and by then she might be making new plans anyway.' Right now she didn't want the cat owners of Church Street to upset Mrs Andrews.

'I don't know about that: it looks like only a matter of time before it happens again.' Tina popped her head round the door to see how Jordan and Bubble were getting on. 'Honestly, Carly, it would break his heart!'

'I know.' As she watched Jordan softly brushing the beautiful long-haired cat, she knew they had to work quickly. Tomorrow she and Liz would call on Mrs Andrews and have another talk. Maybe by the weekend, they would see an improvement in Mr T, then maybe . . . She crossed her fingers, but didn't dare to hope for too much. One thing at a time.

'Patience!' Liz warned as she, Hoody and Carly stood at the door of the old presbytery next evening. 'Mr T may well be on the mend, but don't expect miracles.'

Hoody had hung around the Rescue Centre since school, demanding to know when they were going to see the cat lady.

'Why? What's so urgent?' Carly had asked.

'Nothing. I want to come along, that's all.' He's been deliberately mysterious, had even left Vinny behind in Beacon Street, where he lived with his sister, to make sure that he didn't upset the cats in the churchyard.

And now they were here, listening to Mrs Andrews shuffle down the hallway. From the sloping outhouse roof, two cats looked down on them, padding back and forth as they heard the door open. Carly noticed that one was the sleek black cat they'd seen on their first visit, and one was the rough, tough tabby stray called Half-Tail.

'I bet I know how he lost half his tail,' Hoody said quietly, gesturing back towards the sound of heavy traffic on the road.

The cats jumped silently to the ground as the cat lady appeared on the step.

Mrs Andrews spied them as they curled around her visitors' legs. 'Now, now; I've already given you your supper, you naughty kitties!' Her dry, high voice pretended to be cross. 'Shoo! You know Mr T doesn't like you to go inside the house!'

Carly and Hoody stopped to herd the cats away from the steps. Half-Tail arched his back and hissed. The black cat slunk off across the garden in amongst the graves.

'Miss Hitchens!' The old lady turned her attention to Liz.

'Hutchins,' Liz reminded her.

'And Sally!' Mrs Andrews greeted Carly. She looked surprised to see them.

'Carly.' She blushed and cleared her throat, ready to introduce Hoody. But there was no time. Mrs Andrews rubbed her gnarled hands together with glee and led them down the hall.

'Mr T, we've got visitors,' she called. 'It's that nice vet who gave you your medicine. She's come to see how you are. Won't she be surprised?'

Following in single file, Hoody shrugged at Carly. He raised his eyebrows until they nearly vanished.

'Shh!' she warned. 'It's looking good!' Mrs

Andrews was talking as if Mr T was back on his feet, and she sounded chirpy.

'Best behaviour!' the old lady warned the cat. She paused at the kitchen door and turned to her guests. 'Mr T can be a bit huffy with strangers at first.'

'So he's feeling better?' Liz went ahead into the kitchen.

Carly held up her crossed fingers to Hoody, then followed.

'See for yourself!' Mrs Andrews said proudly.

Carly looked at the wicker chair but the old tomcat wasn't there. She looked under it, then under the kitchen table and all around the stone-flagged floor.

'Not there; here!' Mrs Andrews pointed to the windowsill, the one sunny spot in the room.

And there Mr T sat, his stripy ginger coat gleaming in the sun. His yellow eyes blinked sleepily at them and the end of his tail flicked.

'He can't see you very well,' Mrs Andrews reminded them, 'but he can hear well enough. He knows he has visitors all right.'

'Did he get up there by himself?' Carly asked.

It was a long leap up from the floor to the windowsill.

'He did,' the old lady said proudly. 'And he's got his appetite back.'

Liz smiled and nodded. 'I'll clean his teeth for him while we're here. That'll help clear up his sore mouth.'

'Do you hear that, Mr T?'

The old cat flicked his tail and decided to ignore them. He turned his head to gaze out of the window.

'Shall I go ahead?' Liz asked.

As she gave her permission and Liz got to work with a small, sharp metal hooked instrument, Mrs Andrews drew Carly and Hoody aside. 'Sally, I prayed and prayed for Mr T when he was ill,' she confided. 'And look what a miracle we've got!'

'He looks much better,' Carly agreed.

'Fit as a fiddle already.' She sighed happily. 'He's full of life again, not just stuck in that old chair. Why, I could even think of taking him away from here and moving in with my sister, who would be more than happy to have us, if . . . if . . .'

Her face changed and she sighed.

'If what?' Carly's eyes narrowed. 'Now that Mr T has got this new medicine, he could easily cope with the move.'

Another sigh; this time a deep one. 'It's not Mr T I'm worried about any more. It's all my other kitties!'

'Oh, but you don't have to worry about them!' How could she explain that by stopping feeding them Mrs Andrews was actually doing the neighbourhood cats a great big favour?

'That's all you know about it,' the old lady retorted. 'My kitties rely on me to feed them. How could I bear to know they were going hungry if I left?'

'But they wouldn't go hungry. They already have owners who feed them.'

'That's true. Some do,' Mrs Andrews conceded. 'But not all. Lots of my kitties don't have anyone except me. There's Half-Tail, for instance. He doesn't have a soul in the world to look after him. He lives in the old bell-tower in the church and, apart from the odd mouse he manages to catch, the only food he gets is what I give him. What would happen to Half-Tail if I took Mr T to live with my sister?'

Carly frowned. She'd been so busy hoping that Mr T would get better, she hadn't thought it through. 'I'm sure they'd manage,' she said weakly.

But the only lady wouldn't agree. 'No, my kitties need me here. I couldn't leave them to look after themselves. It wouldn't be a Christian thing to do!' She glanced at Liz working on Mr T's teeth on the table. The cat had submitted to the vet's firm but gentle grasp. Wrapped inside a soft white towel, he let his jaws be opened for his teeth to be scaled.

'Maybe they wouldn't have to look after themselves if you took Mr T to your sister's.' Hoody spoke up. He looked intently at the old lady, leaning forward to tell her his plan.

'Who would feed them?' She shook her head, letting a stray wisp of grey hair fall. 'There's no one else around here who cares for stray cats.'

'Who says they'd have to stay here?'

'What do you mean? Where else would they go?' The frown on Mrs Andrews's lined face deepened. But she too leaned forward, caught by Hoody's eager gaze.

'Somewhere nice and safe,' he whispered. 'A place specially for cats, instead of them having to live rough in the graveyard and on the streets round here. They'd get loads to eat and all the proper jabs and stuff so they didn't catch the flu.'

Carly stared. What was Hoody playing at? Why was he raising the old lady's hopes?

'Where is this place?' Mrs Andrews asked.

'In the country, away from the traffic. Loads of space.' He spread his hands, making it all sound straightforward. 'It's out on the Weygrove Road, then off a side lane, through a village, in the middle of nowhere.'

'But what's it called?' Carly couldn't restrain herself any longer.

'Roman Hill Cat Sanctuary,' he told her. 'Remember I told you I had an idea? Well, I looked up cats' homes in the phone book, rang them and asked if they'd got room for any more strays.'

'What did they say?' She glanced at Mrs

Andrews, whose face had cleared as she clung to
Hoody's every word.

'They said yes, no problem. Bring them over
as soon as we like.'

8

Mrs Andrews thought Hoody was wonderful.
'So clever, so kind!' she cooed. She said she would
never listen again to the bad stories people told
about the youth of today.

A silent, embarrassed Hoody beat a hasty
retreat, but not before Carly had made plans for
the next day, Saturday.

'Meet me at the church gates at nine. We'll
make a start on catching the strays.'

'How will you take them to the sanctuary?' the
old lady asked. 'It must be a long way away.'

Carly had already thought of this. She'd got over the surprise and her mind was moving fast. 'We've got an inspector at Beech Hill called Steve Winter. He'll be able to drive them to Roman Hill in his van. He'll probably help us to round them up as well.'

'Not at nine o'clock tomorrow,' Liz warned. She's finished with Mr T and they were all standing on Mrs Andrews's doorstep, ready to leave. 'I know Steve will be busy then.'

'We'll come anyway,' Hoody said eagerly. 'Steve can come later, once we've caught the cats.'

They agreed on the plan and went their separate ways.

'See you tomorrow, *Sally*!' Hoody laughed, nipping off past the Hare and Hounds before Carly could retaliate.

'Dear Sally and Hoody,' the note began. It was written in spidery ink and pinned to the presbytery door when they arrived early next morning. 'I felt I would rather not be here to see my kitties being taken away today, even though I know that the home they're going to is better than the life they have at present. I said goodbye when I gave them their breakfast this morning. I've gone to visit my sister in Birmingham to discuss arrangements for moving in with Mr T. Back by teatime to give him his supper. Kind regards, Lily Andrews.'

Carly smiled and took down the note. She glanced at the empty dishes of food on the doorstep, then up at the outhouse roof, looking for cats.

'Hang on, what's it say on the back?' Hoody took the paper and read, 'PS: Good luck. PPS: Please take special care of Half-Tail for me. He was my first stray.'

'There he is!' Carly pointed to the roof, where the brown tabby crouched. He stared at them with his hazel eyes, his stocky, striped body ready to pounce, his stubby tail waving crossly.

'OK, let's get started.' Hoody began to arrange the cat carriers that Steve had dropped off for them before he'd gone on to pay his prearranged visit to Sedgewood City Farm. The plan was for the inspector to return with the van in an hour's time.

Carly too got busy. 'I hope these cats are still hungry,' she muttered, opening the wire mesh door of each carrier in turn. She popped a small dish of tempting food inside, then stood back to wait.

'And I hope eight is enough.' Hoody counted the row set out in the overgrown garden.

'We might have to come back a second time.' She fussed and fiddled with the position of the dishes. 'Do you think they'll be able to smell the food all right?'

Hoody looked up at Half-Tail. The stray cat was howling loudly, as if calling the others for a second helping of breakfast. '*He* definitely has, for a start.'

It was time to step back and wait. They crouched quietly in a corner of the garden until two thin shapes came gliding through the churchyard, over the wall and smelling their way towards the food in answer to Half-Tail's call.

Carly saw them and tensed up. One was very young; a tortoiseshell with black and red markings on its back and a soft white belly. The white tip of its tail quivered as it tiptoed forward towards the nearest carrier.

'You or me?' Hoody whispered. From his look-out on the roof, Half-Tail had gone suddenly quiet.

Carly was nearest to the tortoiseshell cat. 'Me!' She would have to wait until the right moment, then move quickly.

'Go on in!' The cat was half-in, half-out of the box. Hoody could see its back-end as the head disappeared inside. 'It's no good; it won't go all the way in.'

'Yes he will.' Carly watched the cat lower its tail and take the nervous last step inside the box. She sprang forward to shut the door and fasten the clasp.

'You did it!' Hoody nodded as the small cat howled from inside the cage. It turned and twisted in the small space, came up to the wire mesh door and peered out.

She gasped and took a deep breath, then lifted the carrier by the handle on top. 'I'm going to put this one inside the church porch until Steve gets here, OK?'

This was also part of the plan; to move each

cat away as they caught it, so that others wouldn't be put off from coming into the presbytery garden for food. She glanced up at Half-Tail, who still stared down from the safety of the roof. 'Don't worry, it won't be for long,' she promised.

She carried the protesting tortoiseshell cat up the moss-covered steps out of the garden and across the churchyard to the stone porch. By the time she'd got back, Hoody had made the second capture of the day and was hurrying towards her with the box. 'Half-Tail's still on the roof,' he said hurriedly. 'He's seen what's going on down here. I don't think we're ever going to get him to come down.'

But other less cautious cats were coming for food; the same mixture of well-cared-for pets and neglected strays that Carly and Hoody had seen before. They watched closely, careful to let the cats with collars come and have their feed then go on their way. A fat white cat came regally across the flat gravestones, whisking her busy tail, the bell on her red collar jingling sweetly. She came and went in her own good time, peering in at the captured cats in the porch, then strolling off across the busy road. Carly followed her to make sure she arrived safely at the other side.

'I'll be glad when this is over and the house is locked up and empty.' She sighed. Every time a cat crossed the road it was lucky to make it. And they were still coming: this time a couple of skinny strays, weaving between a bus and a delivery van that crawled up Church Street. They dodged an overtaking car and scrambled over the churchyard wall, racing now as they smelled the food.

'Both of us?' Carly asked, as the unwary cats dived straight into two carriers and began to gobble.

He nodded. They dived after the cats and closed the doors.

'You can miaow as much as you like,' Carly said, swiftly picking up her box. The prisoner inside cried pitifully to find itself tricked and trapped. 'This is for your own good.'

'Four down, four to go.' Hoody sighed. He legged it back to the presbytery garden. 'Hey, watch it!' Half-Tail had sneaked down while they were away. His stumpy back-end was just backing out of a carrier.

Carly laughed. 'Leave him, Hoody. He deserves to get away with that!' She was amazed how the cat had worked it out so cleverly.

But Hoody had gone in with a flying tackle in an attempt to rush the sneaky cat back into the box.

Too late. Half-Tail turned and saw him. He launched himself sideways, springing over Hoody, who lay full-length on the ground, then he sprinted across the garden, past Carly and across the graves.

'Stop!' she cried. Half-Tail had taken fright. He leaped and launched himself from one gravestone to the next, heading straight for the road.

'On no!' Hoody drew himself up, saw what was happening. He began to run after the fleeing cat.

'No, don't!' It would only scare him more. Carly tried to grab Hoody as he rushed past.

She missed. Half-Tail teetered on the last gravestone before the church gates. His back was arched, his mouth open and hissing. With a quick glance behind at the charging boy, he finally launched himself into the road.

Hoody stopped dead. There was a sudden squeal of brakes, a crunch of metal, then silence.

For a split second Carly closed her eyes. A car door swung open, people came running from across the street. A man was shouting.

'Quick!' she whispered to Hoody, who was still fixed to the spot. He held on to a stone cross, his face white, eyes staring. 'Let's go and see if he's OK!'

Perhaps the car had braked and missed. Half-Tail could have escaped. Praying for a miracle, she ran to the road.

A knot of people had gathered around the front bumper of a blue van. The van was slewed sideways across the road, pointing at the near kerb. A man was spreading his arms in frustration. 'The stupid animal came flying out of nowhere. I never stood a chance!'

Carly's stomach turned. She felt sick. Slowly she sat and let herself slide down from the wall on to the pavement. Everything had gone into slow motion: the man waving his arms, the people shaking their heads as they stared at the ground.

'What happened to it? Did you see?' A woman turned out of the circle to ask Carly.

She ignored her, not even understanding the question.

'Take it easy, love.' The woman came towards her, holding out her hand. 'Was it your cat?'

She shook her head and tried to push through the crowd to see what they were staring at. *Poor Half-Tail. Poor Mrs Andrews. Poor Hoody.*

She expected to see the cat's limp brown body, eyes closed, yet another victim of the Church Street traffic.

But the onlookers were only staring at a small heap of shattered glass, a smashed concrete post, a battered car bumper lying crumpled by the kerb.

'You should control your cat!' The furious driver rounded on Carly. 'Look what it's done to my van!'

'Hang on, she says it's not hers,' the helpful woman explained. She'd taken Carly by the arm and was trying to make her sit down on a bench by the church gate.

'Whose is it, then?' The driver kicked at the wrecked bumper.

'It's a stray,' she whispered faintly.

This only made the man more angry. 'A stray? Who's going to pay for this damage if the stupid thing doesn't even have an owner?' he yelled.

But Carly put her hands over her ears and shook her head. She let herself be led away from the scene of the accident and found herself staring into the kindly eyes of the stranger who'd felt sorry for her. The woman was young, dressed in sports clothes, carrying a rucksack. 'What happened to Half-Tail?' Carly whispered.

'The van driver did hit him,' she said gently. 'He braked hard, but he just caught him.'

Once more Carly's stomach churned. She hugged herself and leaned forward. 'Was it bad?'

'I couldn't tell. I wasn't near enough. But he did get up and run off. It can't have been that bad, can it?'

There was hope, then. 'Which way?' Carly pulled herself back to her feet. She looked frantically up and down the street.

'Under that gate, up the steps towards the church, then I lost him,' the woman told her. She watched Carly steady herself. 'Are you OK?'

'Fine.' She took a deep breath.

'Sure?'

'I will be, thanks.' She had to get away from there.

'Where are you going? You can't get into the church . . . !'

Carly climbed the wall without looking back. She had to go and find Hoody, tell him what had happened.

'. . . It's all locked up . . . No one's been in there since they boarded it up. Come back!'

She ignored the kind woman who called after her. There was only one thing on her mind now: she and Hoody had to find the injured Half-Tail and get him back to Beech Hill as fast as they could.

9

'Hoody!' Carly called his name across the churchyard. In the few minutes since the crash, with its sound of squealing brakes and shattering glass, he seemed to have vanished. 'If you're still here, come out and listen to me!'

Her voice sounded hollow in the silent presbytery garden as she called again and again. 'Hoody, Half-Tail's still alive. We have to find him!'

She saw the four remaining cat carriers still standing in a neat row by the steps, empty reminders of their carefully laid plan. Mrs Andrews's note fluttered across the garden until it caught itself against the thorns of a gnarled rosebush. Behind her, across the churchyard, Carly could hear the faint miaows of the cats they had captured.

'OK!' she shouted, turning suddenly away from the deserted house. 'I'll look for him by myself!' It was typical of Hoody to shoot off without waiting. He would be in a state, blaming himself for the crash, running off to be alone somewhere. *Well, let him.* Half-Tail was what mattered, not Hoody feeling guilty and not being able to stand it.

Half-stumbling against the nearest headstone, Carly stopped to take a deep breath. Where would the poor cat have run to after the accident? The woman had said he'd escaped from under the wheels of the van in the direction of the church. He would be looking for shelter, guided by instinct after the shock of the crash. Somewhere shaded and quiet, away from the terrifying noise.

Inside the church? It was locked and boarded

up, but a small animal might find a gap to creep through. She began to search high and low, checking the blank arched windows, scanning the grimy walls, dizzied by the height of the bell-tower and steeple against a windswept sky.

'This way!' a voice hissed in her ear.

She jumped and whirled round. 'Hoody!'

He grabbed her sleeve and pulled her round to the back of the church. 'I think I've found a way we can climb through. It needs two of us, though.'

'What are you doing? Where have you been?' Carly planted both feet firmly against the edge of a grave and wrenched herself free.

'Looking for Half-Tail,' he said grimly. 'I heard what the woman said.'

'Why didn't you wait? I've been looking every-where!' *Wasting precious minutes, feeling sorry for himself.*

'It's all my fault, isn't it?' He was like a balloon going down, slumping back against the stone church wall, giving in to his guilt.

Carly's emotions seesawed. She stared at Hoody's knitted brows and pale face, then quickly shook her head. 'Not, it's not. It's both of us. And we were only trying to do what was best.'

'But it wouldn't have happened if I hadn't tried to grab him. You told me not to.' Hoody sagged forward, hanging his head.

'Look, it doesn't matter. It's not important. The crash happened and that's all there is to it.' Carly tried everything she could think of to click him back into action. 'Where's this way in that you found?'

'Behind me.' He half-turned his head towards a flat gravestone up against the wall.

So Carly stepped past him and climbed on to it, stretching to find a gap in the boarded-up window behind.

'Not there.' Slowly Hoody followed. He hauled himself from the gravestone up on to a low sloping roof that came out at a right angle from the main building. 'You have to climb up on here.'

'Give me a hand, will you?' She reached out her arm until he pulled her up after him. Then they went on all fours up the slope until they sat astride the ridge of the roof. This porch must have been another way in for the priest.' From this height she could make out a worn and overgrown path cutting across the churchyard from the old house. 'So where's this gap?'

Once more Hoody led the way. 'I saw it the first time we came here,' he explained. 'See that window?'

She followed the line of his pointing finger and picked out a small one with a round arch that must have been forgotten when the windows were boarded up. The wind and the rain, or perhaps stones thrown at it by kids, had battered a hole in the leaded glass. 'You reckon a cat could get through there?'

'From this roof, along that stone ledge.' Hoody sounded sure. There was a jutting-out section carved into the wall, weather-beaten and crumbling, but still wide enough for a cat to balance along.

Carly crouched on the roof of the low out-building, feeling the strong wind tug at her jacket and hair. 'But *we* couldn't,' she pointed out. It was madness to think they could crawl through such a small hole, or even to imagine they could make their way along the narrow ledge.

'I never said we could. I'm just showing you how Half-Tail might have got in.' Balancing carefully, Hoody stood up and turned his attention to the large window nearby. 'I think we can work this board loose,' he told her, beginning to pull at it. The screws that held it in place were rusty and the wood soft and half-rotten from months of rain. 'Give me a hand, Carly.'

Relieved that they weren't going to risk their necks by clinging to the ledge, she set to. She eased her fingers under the board and when Hoody gave the order she pulled hard. The wood splintered but didn't give way.

'Again,' Hoody said. For the moment he'd forgotten about feeling guilty. He took the strain and wrenched at the board.

It splintered a second time and cracked up its length. Carly was left holding a big, jagged piece of broken wood that had come away from the window. Behind it was what they'd been hoping for: an empty window frame. 'What happened to the glass?' she gasped.

'Who cares?' Hoody was already scrambling to see inside. 'It probably got vandalised.'

'Can you see anything?'

No. It's too high.' He lowered himself on to the roof. 'I'll have to give you a leg up so you can climb in.'

'Why me?' For a second she drew back.

'You're lighter than me. And smaller. You can squeeze through.'

Reluctantly she got ready to step on to Hoody's bent knees and reach for the window ledge. 'If I get in, I'll try to unbolt a door from the inside and let you in.'

'OK. Are you up?' He struggled to keep his knee steady as he took her weight.

Carly hauled herself on to the ledge and began to wriggle through the gap. 'Yes, but I can't see a thing. It's dark in here!'

'Keep going. Your eyes will soon get used to it. Can you hear Half-Tail?'

'No.' She twisted her body so that her legs hung down inside the musty, pitch-black church. There was probably a three-metre drop to the floor, so she clung to the ledge and eased herself down, only dropping when her arms were at full stretch. She landed with a jolt, but safe and sound. 'I'm in!' she called back, her voice echoing eerily.

'Great. Try the door to this outbuilding. I'll wait for you there!' Hoody's voice grew fainter as he slid down the roof.

There was no time to be scared of the soft, whispering sounds inside the disused church. It could be bats flitting through the old roof beams, or mice scurrying behind pipes or beneath the heavy wooden pews. Carly made things out as her eyes adjusted to the dark. A crack between the double doors of the back porch where they'd climbed let in a sliver of bright light. She made for it and fumbled to find the bolts that held it shut.

Hoody must have reached the door at the same time. 'Can you do it?' he called from the outside.

'Wait!' Her fingers felt along the smooth, worn edge of the door. 'Here's one bolt!' She tugged at it and felt the cold metal ease and slide.

Hoody pulled impatiently. 'It's still locked!'

'Here's another!' She slid a second bolt sideways and the door swung open. Light flooded in as Hoody joined her. 'What now?'

'Let's hope Half-Tail's in here after all that,' he muttered. The church was huge and empty. It smelt of damp wood and cold, wet stone. There were stacks of old pews set against one wall, even piles of old hymn-books left on a window ledge, and nooks and crannies still too dark to see into.

'That's what the woman told me,' Carly reminded him. It was the only clue they had. As the minutes ticked by, she grew more scared for the injured cat. He needed help, and fast.

'But where exactly?' Hoody crept forward into the central aisle, bumping up against an up-turned wooden chair. 'How are we meant to find one little cat hiding in all this mess?'

'Let's think.' Carly refused to be put off now. 'Remember what Mrs Andrews said about Half-Tail living in the church? Didn't she mention whereabouts?'

'The bell-tower!' He spun round. 'Which way's that?'

'At the back of the church.' She pointed to a stone christening font and a narrow door swinging open beyond. 'That should be it!'

The raced for it, footsteps echoing, squeezing into a narrow stone stairway that led up the tower to an open platform lit by slits in the stonework.

'Stop!' Carly hissed, out of breath after the climb. 'Did you hear that?'

Hoody stared up at thick dangling ropes, high beams, ancient bells. 'No, what?'

'I'm sure I heard something. There it is again!' A tiny mewing sound, coming from up above; the thin, high crying of an animal in pain.

'Yes! I *knew* we'd find him in here!' Hoody's feet thudded across the wooden platform, searching for a way to reach Half-Tail. 'How do we get up?'

Carly couldn't see another flight of steps going higher into the ancient tower. The wooden platform they were standing on seemed to be as far as you could go. 'More to the point, how did Half-Tail get up?'

'Are you sure the sound's coming from there?' The walls created an echo that made it hard to tell.

So they called for the cat and listened again.

Half-Tail's high, answering cry came from far up in the bell-tower.

'Here, Half-Tail! Carly appealed for him to come down. As she peered up into the gloom, following the line of the dangling ropes, she could make out the shape of a giant cast-iron bell fixed to a sturdy wooden frame.

'I bet no one's been up there for over a year!' Hoody whispered. He brushed flakes of falling dirt from his face, peering into the cobwebby darkness.

'Half-Tail, come down!' Carly had found an old metal collection plate on the floor. She picked it up and rattled it, as if she was calling the cat for a feed. 'Come on, I'm sure you can do it!'

'If he could get up there, he can get down again.' Hoody changed position and scanned the inside of the tower from a new angle.

'It doesn't follow,' Carly warned. 'If a cat's frightened, it shins up a tree, say, and gets itself stuck. Maybe that's what's happened to Half-Tail.'

'Hey, I can see him!' Suddenly Hoody grew

excited. 'Come here, Carly. He's up on that beam near the bell!'

'Where?' She craned her neck and peered up. There was a glint of hazel eyes staring back at them, a dark, huddled shape.

'What if he falls off?' Hoody's excitement switched to fear. 'See how narrow it is!'

'Don't worry, cats have fantastic balance.' As Carly tried to keep Hoody calm, looking up at the runaway cat, she felt a drop of moisture fall on to her cheek. She rubbed it and shuddered to see her fingertips had turned bright red. 'Blood!' she gasped.

'And here!' Hoody crouched to point at darker spots on the dusty floor. 'It looks like he's bleeding pretty badly.'

'But how did he get up?' She studied the bare, sheer walls until her frightened gaze came to rest. 'Wait. See that old ladder fixed to the far wall?'

'That's it!' Hoody made it out; some of its rough wooden rungs were broken, but it did lead high into the tower. 'I'm going up to fetch him!' he decided in a flash.

'Oh, be careful!' Carly knew there was no choice. If Half-Tail was bleeding, he might soon grow too weak to balance on the beam. And he was still watching them and wailing out loud, as if he was pleading for help.

She watched Hoody test the bottom rung and set off up the ladder, his skinny frame lit by shafts of light from the slits in the tower. He climbed easily without looking down, stopping to check out a rung that looked rotten or wobbly. Soon he was high above the platform, more than halfway towards rescuing Half-Tail from his dangerous perch.

The cat saw him, stood up gingerly and shuffled a few centimetres further along the beam. He howled as one of his back paws touched the wood, then he let it hang loose over the edge.

'It's OK, he's coming to help you!' Carly wished he could understand. It must look as if Hoody was trying to trap him again. 'Stay where you are!'

Half-Tail stopped and stared. His injured foot threw him off balance. He used his stump of a tail to try to right himself. For a few moments he wobbled unsteadily.

Then Hoody's head came level with Half-Tail's beam. So near . . . Carly saw him let go of the rickety ladder and reach out.

Then a blur. A second of whirling arms, yells, tumbling bodies. Half-Tail's injured foot gave way and he toppled. He fell from the high beam, plummeting towards her. And at that moment, the rung Hoody was standing on cracked and gave way. He cried out and launched himself into space, arms and legs spread-eagled like a parachutist, tumbling down.

10

Above Carly's head, the giant bell swung and rang out with a deafening clang. Hoody had grasped at the bell-rope and caught hold, clinging to it to break his fall.

But Half-Tail still came plunging head first towards her, going limp then twisting in midair until, miraculously, he was the right way up. Carly gasped as he landed square on his feet, howling with pain as the injured leg hit the floor.

The bell swung again, clashing out its warning. As Half-Tail gathered his senses and crept towards her, she glimpsed Hoody descending like a gymnast, swinging crazily on the frayed rope. Carly scooped the cat out of his way and let him slide. He too landed safely, letting go of the thick rope and watching it snake up towards the roof.

Then there were footsteps running across the empty church below, someone shouting their names between the riotous clanging of the giant bell.

'We're up here!' She recognised Steve Winter's voice beyond the whirling chaos of her own thoughts. 'We're in the bell-tower. Everyone's OK!'

Winded and dazed, Hoody struggled to his feet. 'Speak for yourself,' he gasped. He held his arms across his ribs and staggered towards the stone stairs. 'I'm going deaf up here!'

Carly followed him, cradling Half-Tail, who lay quiet and unresisting in her arms.

Clang! Clang! The bell swung to and fro under its own weight, but less frantic now. The peals slowed, each one thundering out across the churchyard on to Church Street and City Road.

'What the . . . !' Steve waited speechless at the bottom of the stairs as first Hoody, then Carly, staggered down.

She held out the frightened cat. 'He was in a car crash, but he escaped and hid up there. Then he fell.'

'Did he land properly?' As always, the Beech Hill inspector stayed calm, quickly leading the way back through the church and out of the open door into the daylight.

'Yes, the right way up,' she told him.

'How?' Hoody couldn't believe that Half-Tail knew which way to land.

Laying the patient in the soft grass, Steve examined him. 'It's normal,' he explained. 'Every cat has this righting reflex. Something to do with crystals and liquid inside the inner ear. It only takes milliseconds for the brain to receive the signal that it's falling, then the cat rights itself, ready to land.'

'So is he OK?' Carly watched Steve examine the bleeding back paw.

'Hold on, give me a chance.' He watched Half-Tail draw his paw away from his touch. 'There may be a broken bone in the foot, but the flesh wound isn't too bad. He was lucky there.' Swiftly taking a surgical sheet from his jacket pocket, Steve laid it flat on the ground and rolled the cat inside it so that only his head peered out.

'What are you doing now?' Hoody crowded round, trying to see.

'Checking his chin. Cats don't have very strong neck muscles, so when they fall from a height they land the right way up but their chins often hit the ground. There might be a midline fracture here too.' Gently Steve eased Half-Tail's jaw from side to side.

'Can we give him first-aid?' Carly pointed to the patch of blood soaking through the sheet from the injured paw. Considering all that the cat had been through, it looked as though he'd got off lightly. But she was worried about the loss of blood.

Steve nodded. Out from his other pocket came a sealed packet containing a lint pad and bandage. 'Strap it up tight,' he told Carly.

So she pressed the pad against the deep cut in Half-Tail's paw while Steve held him tight. Then she wrapped the bandage round it, careful to see that it stayed in place. 'He looks pretty dazed,' she said quietly.

'I'm not surprised.' Slowly Steve was beginning to piece together what had happened. 'So does Hoody there!'

Hoody was still hovering behind them, taking deep breaths and clutching his sides. 'I'm OK,' he assured them. 'Just winded, that's all.'

'Are you sure you don't want us to call a doctor?' The inspector gave Half-Tail to Carly and stood up.

'No way!' Hoody didn't want a fuss. There were the captured strays to collect from the front porch, the empty carriers to be fetched from the presbytery garden and loaded into the Beech Hill van. But Hoody glanced up one last time at the tall tower and the steeple perched on top and heard the old bell still pealing gently after the sudden drama of his fall.

He shuddered, then turned away. 'Come on, what are we waiting for?' he said through clenched teeth. 'We've got to get this cat back to your place before anything else happens!'

*

They prepared a cage for Half-Tail next to Bubble in the peaceful first-floor cattery at the Rescue Centre. Then they fetched the other four strays from the van and found room for them in cages further down the row.

Paul, Liz and Mel had been there to greet them after the end of Saturday morning surgery, and now the nurse lined a cage with a soft, newly laundered blanket while the two vets checked Half-Tail's injuries.

'Nothing to eat just yet,' Paul told Carly as he finished the examination and handed the cat back to her. 'But he can have water to drink.' He looked closely at her to see how she was coping. 'Don't worry, there's just a slight fracture of the bottom jaw that will soon heal itself, and nothing else seriously wrong. The cut on the foot looks worse than it actually is. In fact, I'd say this chap's almost as tough as Bubble there.'

Jordan Smith's Norwegian Forest cat didn't welcome her new neighbour. When she saw Carly slip Half-Tail into the next-door cage, she raised her hackles, then hissed and spat.

'Uh-oh, you can tell someone's nearly ready to go home!' Liz laughed.

'And back to a nice safe situation.' Carly's dad had picked up the latest news from Carly that Mrs Andrews was making arrangements to go and live with her sister. 'It seems that there's not likely to be any cat lady to tempt them over the road. Wait till Jordan hears that!'

'Speaking of Jordan . . .' Liz was at the window looking down over the carpark at the Smith family getting out of their car. 'We can't seem to keep him away!'

'So why not bring him up and tell him the good news?' Paul suggested to the rescuing heroes.

Carly glanced at Hoody. 'You or me?'

'You.'

'Typical.' He never wanted to be in the limelight. Carly grinned as he shuffled into the background. Then she flew downstairs to greet the Smiths.

'. . . You mean, Bubble's going to be safe from now on?' The little boy held her hand as she led him up to the cattery. His mum and dad followed, all smiles.

'She won't have any special reason to cross the busy road. Neither will any of the other cats who live near you.' Carly saw his dark eyes shine as he climbed the stool next to Bubble's cage. 'And the cats from the churchyard who don't have homes are going to live in the country, thanks to Hoody,' she promised.

Jordan nodded. He stole a shy glance at the tall, silent boy hanging about by the door. Then he pushed his fingers through the wire mesh to try to stroke Bubble.

'Here.' Paul moved in to lift the cat out. 'You can hold her if you like.'

They stood back and watched the little boy's face as he turned to sit on the stool.

'Reallly and truly?' A wary look crept over him, as if he thought the soft grey cat might still be too poorly. Then a slow smile spread across his face as Bubble snuggled up to him. Gently he took her on his lap and stroked her long silky grey coat.

The cat purred and folded her feet under her

chest. She curled her bushy tail nice and warm round her body, blinking up at Jordan with her brilliant amber eyes.

From inside his cage, with his bandaged foot and stumpy tail, the tough new arrival rattled his door.

'Jealous!' Carly laughed with the others. She went to keep Half-Tail company. 'But there's no need. Just wait until you hear your new address: Roman Hill Cat Sanctuary, Weygrove.'

'Very posh,' Liz agreed.

'Compared to that old bell-tower,' Hoody couldn't help reminding them.

'And that spooky churchyard.' Carly sighed. From now on, the mournful old place would be left to the mice and the bats. Mrs Andrews would move out with Mr T and the ivy would grow over the presbytery door and the paths would soon be choked with weeds. 'And no more nasty horrible road,' she told Half-Tail and Bubble.

'No more crashes.' Hoody spoke up from the door.

'And no time to stand around here con-gratulating ourselves,' Paul broke in. He listed the jobs still to be done. 'There's a Peruvian guinea-pig about to give birth just down the corridor, half a dozen dog kennels to disinfect, and a white cat called Malibu in reception waiting to be admitted.'

'Just an ordinary day at Beech Hill.' Carly sighed.